CHANGE OF HEART

By Kevin O'Hagan

Grosvenor House
Publishing Limited

This book is published by
Grosvenor House Publishing Ltd
Link House
140 The Broadway, Tolworth, Surrey, KT6 7HT.
www.grosvenorhousepublishing.co.uk

This book is a work of fiction. Any resemblance to
people or events, past or present, is purely coincidental.

A CIP record for this book
is available from the British Library

ISBN 978-1-83975-719-8

Dedication

For family and friends no longer with us. Thank you for being in my life and leaving so many beautiful memories behind.

Other Books by the Author

Battlescars

No Hiding Place

Last Stand

Killing Time

Author's note

Some cities, towns and locations mentioned in this novel exist in real life.

Landscapes, businesses, streets, and layouts take on another imaginary life in this book. Thank you for indulging me to help in creating this storyline.

Acknowledgements

This book was written in the second major lockdown of the UK due to Covid 19. Once again, the lockdown focused me on my writing and helped me keep disciplined through some tough times.

The seeds for this story were sown a while ago when I watched a television programme introduced by the legend that is William Shatner, forever immortalised as Captain James Kirk of 'Star Trek' fame.

The programme was called *Weird or What*. It is a collection of strange and unexplained events or incidences.

One of the stories on this episode was about *'cellular memory'*, a medical theory that heart transplant victims can inherit their donor's personalities.

I thought, what a great theme for a story, and little by little a plot began to develop, which eventually resulted in this book.

I hope you enjoy the story weaved from this theory as much as I enjoyed writing it.

I thank once again my wonderful daughter Lauren for her proof-reading skills and advice on how grammatically to bring this story together and also, my incredibly talented son Tom for the amazing cover design.

As always, big love to my wife Tina for her continued support of my writing.

Also thank you to Grosvenor Publishers for once again helping guide me through the publishing process to get my manuscript into book form.

God bless you all and I hope that 2021 ends on a better note for us.

Kevin.

Medical Phenomenon

Cellular memory

Definition: cellular memory, is the idea that memories and personality traits can be stored in any individual cells or in other organs, not just in the brain…

'Personality changes following heart transplantation, which have been reported for decades, include accounts of recipients acquiring the personality characteristics of their donor….
   For better or for worse maybe?'

Prologue

So much blood everywhere.

I used to be squeamish when it came to blood. As a child, I was terrified when I accidentally cut a finger or scraped a knee.

I hated going to the dentist for fear of a tooth being pulled and the very thought of an injection made me feel queasy.

I remember going to A&E aged 14. I had been playing football for my school team and I cracked skulls with an opposition player when we both jumped to head the same ball.

After the collision, I fell to the ground in pain and immediately felt the warm trickle of blood down my face.

I began to hyperventilate and go into a state of panic, believing I was about to die as the blood from my head wound flowed faster.

In hospital, I received five stitches. The wound was not going to claim my life after all, but that didn't stop my fear of spilling the good old claret.

I feared confrontation and violence in case somebody bloodied my nose or split a lip.

I managed to hang around with tougher boys by giving them sweets, trading cards or my dinner money, just so I would be protected from the bullies.

I was diagnosed in my late teens as having *hemophobia*, an irrational fear of blood.

I took comfort in eating junk food and reading comics whilst my friends played rugby or trained in martial arts.

I avoided all contact sports like the plague and spent most of the time locked away in the sanctuary of my bedroom.

I desperately wanted to be one of the boys, but I ended up being viewed as a bit of a wimp and an academic rather than a macho man.

In the cinema or on television, I watched Eastwood, Bronson and McQueen. Later, Stallone, Willis and Schwarzenegger. How I longed for their characters' courage, strength and lack of fear.

I craved to have the bottle and ability to smash my bullies into the dust but...

Fear of blood was one of my many childhood hang-ups that carried on into adulthood.

Fear of heights. Fear of water. Fear of public speaking. Fear of the opposite sex.

The list went on. Some I got over with time and maturity.

But the fear of blood is one that has stayed with me all my life.

I couldn't even watch my two children being born. The shame and humiliation of it all.

My wife never forgave me.

What a disappointment I was to her.

Why couldn't I be a 'Dirty Harry' or a 'John Rambo' instead of a mash up of Shaggy and Scooby Doo?

But here's the thing. In recent years, this fear – and many others – have inexplicably gone.

Well, maybe not inexplicably as I suspect it is down to what happened to me and how it has changed me dramatically.

That began three years ago now and so much has happened since that I sometimes don't believe it myself.

I have no control over my new feelings and urges. I truly haven't. But I would rather live a day as a tiger than a lifetime as a sheep.

I had no idea what I was missing until the lifechanging incident.

I realised that, up until then, I had been surviving and not living.

Well, that has changed now.

I am no longer that wimp.

I am no longer Mr Average.

I am a fucking badass.

Things have escalated beyond my control.

People will finally know who I am and recognise and remember my name.

Fame or infamy? Hero or villain?

I will let the public judge that.

So much blood everywhere.

I now look around one last time at the carnage before me. The dead bodies. The acrid smell of cordite and the coppery tang of blood.

How do I know these people around me are dead?

Because I have just killed them.

Yes, little old me.

I will let you into a secret. I enjoyed it.

I felt euphoric.

I have never had a feeling like that in my whole life.

Nothing compares or even comes close to it.

I am glad I experienced it.

So much blood everywhere. Did I mention I used to hate blood...

CHAPTER ONE

Simon

My name is Simon Winter. My life had been unremarkable really until three years ago when I suffered a massive heart attack whilst pulling into a service station on the M4.

I was lucky that I had a work colleague travelling with me that day. He made the call to the emergency services immediately and it saved my life. If I had been travelling alone, I would not be here to relate my story.

You would think that I should be over the moon to have survived, but some days, I question this. It can be a curse and a blessing.

Let me go back in time and tell you how it all happened…

I was travelling back from Cardiff to my home city of Bristol on a grey and rainy Friday afternoon when I suddenly experienced gripping pain in my chest and left arm that travelled to my neck and jaw.

I hadn't been feeling particularly well all day, but I couldn't really pinpoint why. I just felt under the weather.

Thank God I hadn't been in the fast lane.

Fortunately, although I hadn't been feeling 100%, I was just pulling into the services for a Big Mac meal and a large Coke when it occurred.

Well, it was Friday, and I was celebrating the fact that I had just signed up three new clients that wanted to sell their houses.

I was in such a good mood I was going to even buy my passenger, new trainee Callum Fudge, a meal as well.

Oh yes, I forgot to mention that I work as an estate agent.

I work for a company called *Sanctuary Homes*. You may have heard of us.

We did a big advertising campaign on television a few years back.

'*A house is not just a home; it is a Sanctuary.*'

Remember?

Now my timid background might not suggest that being an estate agent was the best of jobs. But it worked as I could hide my real persona behind the cheeky chappy that I had invented over time.

Anyway, I drive a lot with my work. I work mainly in Wales, but live in Bristol, England, so I commute over the Severn Bridge most days.

It's not so bad now that they have taken those damn toll booths away.

I don't mind driving. I like my own company and I enjoy listening to the radio. Not that Radio One shite though. In my opinion, that station hasn't been any great shakes since good old Simon Bates left in 1993 along with his *Golden Hour* and *Our Tune*.

Radio Two is my station of choice. A good mix of old, modern, and classic tunes, plus *PopMaster*, which I always try to listen to.

Anyway, I digress.

Since I left school at 17 years of age, my jobs have been office-based or also involve driving so at the ripe old age of 42, I have certainly piled on the pounds.

I didn't really enjoy exercise as a young adult for many reasons, so the thought of going into a gym now at my age with a load of muscle boys and lithe, frighteningly toned babes didn't appeal.

I know all gyms aren't like that these days, but the prospect of an octogenarian running faster than me on a treadmill was also horrifying.

I don't really play sports and haven't done for a long time. I played a bit of football when I was younger but that was it. Unless you class pool, snooker, and darts as an active pastime. I am what you might term a couch potato.

I hated going out to pubs or clubs in the city centre as I feared violence. I lived like a timid animal, always in a state of anxiety just in case an apex predator came along.

I had grown up into a big lump, but I was soft as shit and gutless. I hated myself for this, but I couldn't change.

The only thing I could have a good fight with was a giant sausage roll or an 18-inch pepperoni pizza.

My doctor did warn me to lose some weight as my last health check confirmed I was clinically obese, had high blood pressure and cholesterol and was borderline type 2 diabetic.

So did my previous check though.

I looked suitably shocked and disgusted with myself and left vowing that I would head to Sports Direct immediately and kit myself out with the latest in tracksuit and trainers. Then I would hit the pavements and park jogging each day.

Who was I kidding?

I also promised I would venture down the health food aisles of my local Asda.

This honestly would have been on a par with me thinking about trekking to the North Pole.

Ryvita, cereal bars and almond milk didn't float my boat.

Names such as Atkins, Paleo, Ketogenic and 5:2 frightened the shit out of me.

A vegan to me was somebody out of *Star Trek*.

My diet is rubbish. I am the takeaway king and a junk food junkie.

Well, when you go home to an empty flat at the end of a day, what is the point in cooking?

Deliveroo has become my constant and welcoming mistress on dark lonely nights or any type of night.

The interior of my car looks like somebody has tipped the contents of the rubbish bin of my local 7/11 into it.

I should really be sponsored by Greggs or Cadbury. I am a walking advert for them.

Whilst driving I have made more pitstops than Sir Lewis Hamilton; only mine are at a network of strategically placed service stations, all bearing the heart-warming and seductive branding of Costa, Burger King, Nando's and Crispy Kreme.

I am unashamedly what you would call a fat bastard if you were allowed to call anybody a fat bastard these days without being arrested by the politically correct squad.

My good mate and drinking buddy Greg Badcock still calls me a fat bastard though, but that is okay because he is a fat bastard as well, so we are in a specialist club of fat bastards.

Currently, there is a fucking waiting list to get in this club.

I do like a beer or six. Oh, and the odd glass of wine. I am also rather partial to a drop of Jack as well.

I think that is it, except my 20-a-day habit of smoking Lambert and Butler's. It has been a habit since 1993 when I was 14 years old.

Mary O'Brien took me behind the school bike sheds to do something naughty with me. Or so she led me to believe.

Mary O'Brien was hot and one of those early developed girls if you get my drift. I was a nerd. But here I was with the wonderful creature alone together.

Was I dreaming this, and at any moment now would wake up in my bed to bitter disappointment and my pyjamas bottoms feeling slightly damp in the groin area?

But no, this was for real.

When we got behind the bike shed, imagine my surprise when she produced a packet of Embassy No. 6 and asked me if I wanted a fag. I had to get her to repeat the question again in case by some beautiful, unimaginable mistake I had misheard her. But alas no.

So, with my young, eager, and totally inappropriate erection wilting in my Tesco Value brand grey school trousers, I sparked up and instantly became addicted.

No vapes for me.

Have you ever walked behind a vaper when they have a puff?

It looks like their heads have spontaneously combusted and then you get a sickly whiff of cherry, grape or apricot.

Give me good old nicotine flavour every time.

Yes, when you look at it, I was an ideal candidate for a heart attack. In fact, if Simon Cowell had invented a show entitled *X Factor: The Heart Attack*. I would have won it hands down or at least fought it out with Rick Waller. Remember him?

By now you must be getting the picture. If I were a car, I would fail the M.O.T spectacularly and be sent to the breaker's yard.

In my defence, I always had the best of intentions, but I never followed them through.

When every new year came around, I would solemnly vow that this was the year I would clean up my act and get back on track, but something always prevented me from doing so, normally the opening of another Pizza Hut.

My wife Jean finally got fed up with all my useless procrastinating and left me, taking our two children Harry and Chloe with her.

They were the only two good things that came out of our marriage.

We had fallen out of love long before Jean decided enough was enough.

Since the birth of Chloe, we didn't share the same bed together and she is eight now.

I remember telling Jean once after we had some new wardrobes fitted in the master bedroom that the fitter from Sharps Bedroom Specialists had been in our bedroom longer than I ever had.

The joke went down like a lead balloon.

For a while, I did look to seek solace in the arms of a woman who worked in the estate agent's office, Brenda Burns. She was no looker but tended to put it around a bit and wasn't fussy who she put it around with. She also enjoyed a good takeaway.

The relationship didn't last long as the two times we went to bed together I couldn't perform.

I was softer than a Mr Whippy's ice cream left out in the sun.

You would have thought somebody had dipped my dick in Lenor.

I mentioned this to the doctor when I had the health check-up and he told me it was all probably down to my lifestyle choices, stress, and the fact I was a fat bastard. Well, he didn't exactly use those last words, but you get the picture.

Did I heed the warning? No, and luckily for me, to save any more embarrassment, shortly after my second non-performance with Brenda, she was transferred to our Bath City branch. Thank God for that.

I wouldn't miss her, well maybe her homemade spag bol. That was the dogs.

So, you can see, I am not in great shape in any sense of the word and the heart attack was the icing on the cake.

As I pulled my Ford Mondeo into the parking area of the service station, I gritted my teeth and told a frightened looking Callum to ring 999.

I prayed he knew how to do this as, in all the times he had been in the car with me, he had just texted or trawled through Instagram and Snapchat on his mobile.

As a typical 17-year-old, I wondered if he had ever used the phone to make an actual call.

Thankfully, he did know, but by the time I could hear the sirens approaching, I had slipped into unconsciousness.

Later, I learnt that I had technically died twice. Once at the scene and once in the ambulance.

I have been asked since what did it feel like and did, I see myself being drawn to a light down a tunnel?

I can tell you I honestly don't remember a thing until I woke up in a hospital bed with various wires and tubes sticking out of me.

My life hadn't flashed before me, which could have been a blessing. Otherwise, I may have not wanted to come back from the other side.

But back I came.

Was I glad?

I am not sure. I was just feeling numb.

I had been taken to Southmead Hospital in Bristol where they cared for me.

When I was somewhat better, a Doctor named Mr. Kumar looked after my recovery.

I must admit, when he first introduced himself, I was tempted to ask if he still lived at number 42 but thought better of it.

At least I hadn't lost my sense of humour.

He patiently explained that I had survived a massive heart attack. He went on to say that I was now stable, but there were complications.

Mr. Kumar told me that I had a heart attack because my coronary arteries had become blocked. This stops the blood supply to the heart's muscles, meaning it can't get the oxygen it needs. Starved of oxygen, the heart can't pump properly, and, in severe cases, it may effectively stop beating altogether, which can kill you.

Which in my case it nearly did twice...

He continued to inform me that damage to the heart muscle can lead to heart failure. When your heart can no longer pump blood around your body normally. This leads to symptoms such as swelling of the ankles and shortness of breath, which can affect you for the rest of your life and often become progressively worse. Although there are prescription drugs that can help limit the impact of heart failure, there isn't a cure at present.

I listened to what he had to say and then asked what the solution was. I must admit he had got me scared.

Mr. Kumar told me he was going to recommend me for a heart transplant as basically the one I had was worn out and another cardiac arrest was probably imminent and next time I might not be able to be resuscitated.

I thought at that moment if he continued with this frightening news, I might well have the next heart attack there and now.

I was shaking like a shitting dog; I can tell you.

He said he would contact one of the specialist cardiac hospitals and put me on the waiting list marked urgent to see if they could get me a match as soon as possible.

I could go home soon. I was advised to take things steady. I was also told to try and lose some weight, stop smoking and cut out alcohol. Gentle walking would be fine.

Shit, I felt like somebody had just castrated me.

I was put on a host of medications mainly with names starting with anti-something. Most I couldn't pronounce and, to be honest, I didn't care.

I was in shock and much of what I was being told tended to fade in and out of my consciousness like an old radio signal.

Simon Winter having a heart transplant at 42 years of age. Shit. What the fuck had I done to my body? This was serious.

Family and friends visited with sympathy, flowers, and grapes when, to be honest, I would rather have had a double Jack Daniels on the rocks.

My younger sister by two years, Sue, God bless her, told me I could come and stay with her until the operation, but I declined her kind offer. She had three kids and her husband Joe worked night shifts on the docks. They didn't need me under their feet.

I would be alright at my flat. The neighbours either side of me were sound and had already visited me saying that they would be only too happy to help in any way they could when I came home.

A cardiac nurse would also be assigned to pay me daily visits.

I thanked them all, but inwardly, I was ashamed of myself.

My wife Jean and the kids visited me once.

I hated Harry and Chloe to see me like this and I told Jean that it was better that they didn't come in again.

She agreed but said that she would keep in touch via phone or Skype.

Much water had gone under the bridge since our separation.

I knew she was seeing somebody else.

A bloke called Tommy Norris. He drove a delivery van for Iceland.

Jean's chest freezer was well stocked at home these days.

Apparently in his spare time he ran marathons which contrasted with me who only ate them or *Snickers* as they are now known.

Obviously being as fit as a butcher's dog meant it wasn't only Jean's freezer that was getting filled regularly.

I met him once when I went around the house to pick up the kids for a Saturday afternoon visit to the zoo.

I hated to admit it, but he was a nice guy. Polite and inoffensive. I liked the skinny little fucker.

He treated Jean and the kids well.

I was happy for Jean. She deserved it. I hadn't been much of a husband.

My worked had ruled my life. Married life hadn't really been for me. We had both been too young.

The thought of going home every night to a wife and two young children, dirty nappies, feeding bottles and all the other shit that went with it hadn't really appealed to me, so I choose the pub, a takeaway, and my mates instead.

I had been a selfish bastard.

Before leaving my bedside, Jean had told me to look after myself and wished me luck.

I saw pity in her eyes which I hated.

Then, like the Jean of old, her parting shot was that she had told me far too many times that this would happen sooner or later and that I was a stubborn bastard.

I couldn't hate her for that because she was right.

My dear old mum, God rest her soul, who passed away last year, had also told me umpteen times over the years to lose weight.

My dad had died of a heart attack at age 55. He was pulling up some carrots on his allotment for Sunday dinner when he keeled over.

I remember the old joke of this happening to a man and his next-door neighbour, when hearing the terrible news, asked his wife whatever did she do? The wife told her she opened a tin of peas.

Seriously though, my dad was not exactly what you would call svelte. It did shock me for a long while and made me think about my own mortality.

But with time, the memories fade and you go back to your old habits.

Mum always reminded me of what happened to Dad, and I half-heartedly agreed with her whilst chomping away on one of her legendary bacon butties.

I thought I was invincible. Live for the moment. That was my motto. The years went on and so did the weight.

I began to avoid mirrors. The bathroom scales gathered dust in the back of the wardrobe.

My belly went gradually from resembling a flabby pink bum bag to looking nine months pregnant.

It was so big my dick became like an old friend that you didn't see except birthdays and Christmas.

I can't remember the last time I had a bath.

It would have been a trial getting in and if I did manage this monumental task, I wouldn't have been able to get out of the fucker, so I stuck to showers.

My ass was getting so big the cheeks had their own separate post codes.

All the signs were there, particularly recently, but I chose to ignore them.

I remember last summer taking the kids down to Weston Super Mare, a seaside resort 30-odd miles from Bristol.

It was a beautiful day and they played on the beach and swam in the sea.

Whilst playing football with them on the beach, I found that I was constantly breathless, and any sort of running had me panting like a dog on heat.

To save face, in the end I called a stop to play and suggested ice creams.

Inwardly, I was guilt-ridden that I was so unfit and not able to play with my children. Christ, I was only in my early forties and here I was wheezing like a pensioner who had worked all their life in an Asbestos factory.

I must admit, some mornings I found myself puffing from just putting on my socks or doing up my shoelaces.

As my waistline got bigger so did my trousers.

Shirts, tees, jumpers became XXL.

No shape and no style.

I resembled a man stood behind an ironing board looking over a pile of washing.

When I hung my clothes out on the line, I am sure we lost an hour's daylight.

I kidded myself I would be alright. I always used humour and acted the clown to hide my concerns.

Well, I'm not alright.

I am not whinging about it, mind you.

If you choose to live your life in a certain manner, you must take the consequences that go with it. Good or bad.

That's Karma for you.

I had now become one of the people I always used to bleat on about. The ones who stuff themselves to obesity. The ones who own a Greggs loyalty card and lovingly fondle it like it was an American Express platinum credit card.

I am now the person sat on the sofa chomping down a giant pizza or a family size bag of crisps telling anybody who cared to listen that I didn't give a fuck how fat I was, but then when things went pear-shaped, I was crying and sobbing for the NHS to bail my lardy ass out and help me.

What a wanker I was.

But I swear here and now I will change if I get through this operation.

I swear on my kids' lives, I WILL change.

CHAPTER TWO

Eddie

I am stood on the front door of *Bubbles* nightclub in the city centre of Bristol. This is the most popular and busiest club in the Southwest of England.

We get a lot of people through the doors, and it is a melting pot for individuals from all areas of the city.

The club sees all sorts and sometimes that leads to trouble, which means you must have a good team on the door led by the head doorman who knows what he is doing. A person who can handle the heat and if it becomes violent can also handle himself. That person is me.

My name is Eddie Prince. You may have heard of me? I am an ex-boxer. No, nothing to do with playing computer games.

I mean I was a fighter. I boxed professionally at light heavyweight since my early 20's with mixed success. I then moved to cruiserweight, the next weight division up and I did well. I won British and European titles before getting a world title shot in 2003.I was 27 years of age and had been boxing since I was eight years old.

I got my shot against a boxing legend, James 'Lights out' Toney, at Caesars Palace, Las Vegas.

Not bad for a boy from Stepney, East London.

Toney had held world titles at middle, super middle, light heavyweight, and cruiserweight at the time. Later he also went on to even win a version of the heavyweight title. As I said, this man was a legend.

I was in awe of the champ and could not believe on that night, 24th August 2003, that I stood in the ring facing him.

Did I win? Do a Rocky Balboa? Lift the title? Unfortunately, not.

I did go eight rounds with him though until he caught me with a peach of a left hook. It was the hardest single punch I have ever been hit with. They didn't call him 'lights out' for nothing. To my credit, I tried to get back up, but I couldn't beat the count.

I was proud of my achievements, even though I lost. I did lose to a great champion and to share the ring with him was an honour.

A rematch wasn't on the cards, so I took some time out, but eventually, went back to the ring.

But it was a hard slog working my way back up the rankings, especially as I lost my next two fights on points.

I boxed on for a while after, but never reached those heady heights again.

At the age of 32, I retired in 2006. I was losing my speed and my edge. I didn't want to become one of those guys that end up a punch bag for some up-and-coming youngster.

I got out pretty much unscathed.

I have the obligatory broken nose and some scar tissue around both eyes, but people still refer to me as ruggedly handsome, which I will take.

After retiring, I got some offers of TV work. The usual fare appearing as a game show panellist.

I did *Big Brother* and I was also due to appear in the jungle on *I'm a Celebrity*, but I broke my hand in a stupid unlicensed fight that I should have refused.

I knocked my opponent out in the second round, but it blew my chances of some great exposure on what was one of the biggest shows on TV at the time. My agent was not best pleased.

After that, work began to dry up. I had squeezed as much mileage out of my boxing career as possible. People were getting bored with the same old tales I was telling and frankly, I was tiring a little of being the butt of some wise-cracking game show host jokes who I could have punched out in seconds if I wanted.

I thought I might like a crack at acting. I had seen ex-sportsmen like Vinnie Jones become successful from playing tough guy roles and I thought I could do that.

Then an incident changed all of this.

I was in a pub in central London celebrating a good friend's birthday. I don't drink alcohol, never have, but my friend and some of the other lads with us were well oiled and becoming a little noisy and boisterous. Nothing heavy, but it drew the attention of the doormen.

Two of them approached our table. One was a mountainous black guy with a mouthful of gold teeth. The other was white and nearly as big. He sported a teardrop tattoo under his left eye. Both of them looked handy geezers.

The black man asked us politely to keep the noise down; otherwise, we would have to leave.

We were all cool with that and apologised, except one of our party. A guy I didn't know called Harry. He had been a bit of an asshole all evening. Always taking the piss and trying to wind people up. The sort of person normally I would avoid going out with as the more he drank the more of a liability he became. But this wasn't my birthday. I didn't invite him.

As the two doormen were just walking off, this Harry guy said loudly enough for them to hear what a pair of wankers they were.

As a couple of the other lads tried to shut him up, the two doormen returned to the table.

The black man told us it was time to leave.

Harry began to protest, but I told him to drink up and shut up and let's move on.

As we were escorted to the door and shown out, Harry, still spoiling for trouble, had turned around to the two doorman and told them they were both queers and he bet neither of them had a good fight in them.

Again, the black man told us to move Harry on and that was the last warning.

As we made to walk away, Harry, fuelled up on alcohol and later we found out cocaine, broke free and ran up to the doormen posturing and calling them out.

This, time the white guy stepped forward and, without warning, hit Harry on the chin with a crushing right cross.

Harry dropped to the floor like a dead thing.

He had deserved a slap, but Harry must have been giving away five stone in weight to this guy. The ferocity of the punch had nearly separated his head from his shoulders.

The other lads piled forward, and chaos ensued as they started swinging punches at the doormen.

As it was, both of these men could fight and two more of our group hit the pavement and were sleeping like babies.

I stepped in to break up the fight, but the white guy swung a punch at me. I instinctively ducked under it and came up and planted a peach on a left hook on his jaw. His legs turned to jelly as he staggered back, and I followed in with a right cross to his chin.

He hit the pavement, but unknown to me at the time, as he did, the back of his head connected with the bottom concrete step of the stairs leading into the club.

The black guy grabbed me in a bear hug from behind, but by now, I had gone into fighting mode. I smashed the back of my head into his face twice breaking his nose. As his grip loosened, I drove my elbow back into his solar plexus. He released his hold on me and I span quickly hitting him with a right cross/ left hook combination. He went down like a wounded buffalo.

It was all over. The incident had drawn a crowd. The manager of the pub had called the police. I heard somebody shout out in the crowd, "Isn't that Eddie Prince, the ex-boxer?" I had been named and shamed.

The police herded us up and into a back of a van for what we presumed would be a night in the cells and an appearance in front of the Magistrate's Court on Monday morning.

Harry was the only one not put in the van as he was put in the back of an ambulance with severe concussion.

The horror of the whole accident dawned on me when brought into the police station and interviewed.

The white doorman I had chinned named Neville Scott had died from head injuries sustained in the fight. I was looking at a murder charge.

In fact, it ended up as involuntary manslaughter, but I still did four years in Wormwood Scrubs.

I got treated alright inside. I was a bit of a celebrity, but I still lost my liberty over an incident I only stepped into initially to break up.

When I came out, I was like a leper. My television days were well over, and any dreams of Hollywood had died.

Nobody wanted to know me, except the tabloids looking for an exclusive.

I gave it to them, I needed the money, but after that, I found myself pretty much isolated.

They say in times of trouble you find out who your true friends are, and I certainly did.

Once the money and celebrity go so do the hangers-on, off to leech onto the next unexpecting sucker.

I tried to stay positive. I didn't go down the road that many retired boxers choose. The road of alcohol and drugs.

I kept myself fit. I was in the gym most days and also out running. Training kept me going. I even thought about boxing again but getting a license would be difficult if not impossible.

In this period of time, I lost both of my parents to heart failure. Mum first at 70 and then Dad later at 78.

I missed them both terribly. They were my most avid fans when I was boxing, and I remember how I paid for them to have a holiday in America after watching me fight for the world title in Las Vegas. I put them up in Caesars Palace in one of their executive rooms. They were over the moon. They thought they were royalty.

It was the least I could do for them both. They had supported my boxing career from its early days. They were always there for me through thick and thin.

I was their only child, although I did have a sister who was tragically stillborn a few years after me. My parents called her Ruby.

Mum couldn't have any more children after this, so they invested all their time in me.

Don't get me wrong, coming from humble beginnings in East London, I certainly wasn't spoilt, but I was loved and cared for.

A couple of years before Mum's passing, I bought my parents a bungalow in Essex out by the sea so that they could enjoy their retirement.

Although their time there was brief, they had loved it.

Mum was devastated when I went to prison and couldn't face coming to see me in there. Dad came every visit and always brought me something. Usually some of my Mum's home-made cake or biscuits.

I was absolutely gutted when they both had passed away.

I began to regularly run marathons for the Heart Foundation charity and raised thousands to support their cause.

I next decided to donate my heart to medical science when I died. It seemed the right thing to do.

I wanted to give something back. Something which would matter.

When I was at my peak in boxing, a lot of money came my way and I spent it like water. Women, fast cars and gambling became my vices.

I was put on to a few investment deals in property which looked good at the time, but then the big crash of 2008 came, and everything went tits up. I lost it all.

The well was dry.

I had one trade all my life and that was boxing. I was always a bit of a tearaway as a kid. Always getting into fights and involved in petty thief.

I left school with no qualifications to speak of and at the time, seeing as I wanted to become a professional boxer, I didn't think I needed them.

But I wasn't going to become a pro overnight, so I took on labouring jobs on building sites. I kept fit and strong hod carrying and digging trenches. I also did some tarmacking on the motorways.

It was decent enough money, but my parents really wanted me to have a trade, but I was only interested in boxing.

But now it had all come back to bite me on the ass.

The good times had come to an end and so had the money. The prospect of stacking shelves in Tesco or delivering pizzas didn't appeal to a man who once boxed in Vegas for a world title.

When you reach the bottom in sport or the showbiz world, it becomes a lonely place. All the people that were going to help you disappear into the horizon. When you are yesterday's news, nobody wants to know you.

To make ends meet, I took a job as a doorman on one of the clubs in Soho. It was decent enough money and I also got to use the only skills I knew.

I was ever mindful of the situation that brought me prison time and tried to solve problems without my fists, but old habits die hard.

So many people when they have the demon drink inside them become assholes that can't be reasoned with and just won't get out of your face until you chin the bastards. I was good at that.

Many of the people who frequented the club remembered me from my boxing days. Most wanted a selfie or an autograph, some others came to test my reputation. Most of them couldn't fight sleep.

To earn some extra cash, I am not proud to say I got involved selling drugs for a while. This is not a good business to be involved in and I even began carrying a shooter which wasn't my style.

I managed to walk away from this side of my life when the man I was working for was found stabbed to death in his flat.

I was relieved to get out of it all unscathed.

I was developing quite a reputation on the doors and another big club poached me and made me head doorman. More responsibility and more money. I promised myself I would clean up my act.

As I said, when it came to training, I was a disciplined performer. I was still my fighting weight and looked after my health.

But everybody has a personal weakness or an Achilles heel. I still had two: gambling and women. The second was easily available on the doors.

I took a different girl home every weekend.

The gambling came from my glory days.

I even once part-owned a racehorse, but finally sold my shares when I found out I could probably run faster.

Cockney Flyer was definitely the wrong name for this horse.

I mainly still gambled on the nags. The problem was I am not particularly good at it.

As fast as I earnt money, I was frittering it away at Epsom or Sandown.

As I mentioned, I did like the ladies. I was a player flitting from one girl to the next, but that all stopped when I met Ester.

It was a busy Saturday night on the door of *Jester's*, the nightclub that I worked at.

A long line of punters queued to get in. I spotted Ester near the front of the line, and I believe I actually fell in love with her there and then.

She was a stunningly attractive blonde, but not in the stereotypical Barbie doll image.

Ester looked cool and sophisticated in a stylish black trouser suit.

She wore only a touch of make-up, but looked naturally beautiful.

There were two other women with her, and they were all chatting excitedly.

As she came to the front of the queue, I stepped forward and said good evening.

I told her that I had to check her handbag.

She opened her bag for me to inspect and we accidentally touched hands.

It felt like an electric shock had gone up my arm and into my whole body.

Our eyes met and something unsaid passed between us.

By the end of the night, I had asked for her phone number and, a week later, we were dating.

This truly was the only time in my life I *was* punching above my weight.

Ester Thomas came into my life like a breath of fresh air.

She wasn't the usual type of girl I went for. Then in fairness, I probably wasn't the usual type of bloke she went for. But for some reason, we clicked.

Ester was smart, funny and ambitious.

She had a degree in graphic design and worked for a large advertising company.

I felt so inadequate beside her, although she never made me feel this way.

She accepted me for who I was.

I told her about my boxing past and my prison time, but she never judged. She told me that she was only interested in the Eddie Prince now.

Within a month of meeting, I was living with Ester in her Basingstoke flat.

Some people said I had landed on my feet and was sponging off her, but this was never true. I loved her unconditionally.

I had never had a proper relationship and never been in love, but now I was smitten.

Ester told me on more than one occasion to give up the door work and that she was earning plenty of money for us both. But I am old school. I couldn't have a woman being seen to be keeping me, so I carried on with my job. Plus, I enjoyed it. I loved the camaraderie and sense of belonging I got doing it.

Unknown to Ester, though, I still also carried on with my gambling and had now stupidly got myself in debt with a pretty heavy geezer.

Archie Castle. A nasty piece of work.

He ran a money lending and debt collecting business in the area, amongst other things.

When you went to him, this was not the listening bank.

If you didn't pay back what you owed, the interest was astronomical.

If you stalled on a payment or failed to produce the money, you usually got something broke if you were lucky.

You only went to blokes like Castle when you were desperate, and I was.

I had been at the point in my life where I had three bookmakers in the area after my blood for unpaid gambling debts owed to them.

Archie had willingly lent me the money after outlining his business agreement.

He made it clear in no uncertain terms.

I, unfortunately, had failed to keep that agreement.

Castle was beginning to tighten the screws on me, and I wouldn't be able to put him off much longer.

I could have asked Ester for the money, but I was too ashamed of myself. What would she think of me? Her being a successful businesswoman and her bloke being a pathetic waster.

I just didn't have the heart to tell her.

Gambling, like any addiction, is a killer. You just can't stop even when you are fully aware of the consequences.

I had been so disciplined in the ring, but outside of it, I was freefalling to self-destruction.

Then a solution came out of the blue.

One night, Ester told me she had been offered a big promotion in the company she worked for. I was over the moon for her.

She then told me the job was in Bristol and it would mean leaving London and relocating there.

The job also included a fully furnished flat on the city's Harbourside.

In normal circumstances, this would have thrown me a curve ball, but with Archie Castle breathing down my neck, relocation to the West Country seemed an ideal solution.

When the time came to go, I just up sticks and left London without telling a soul, except the manager of *Jester's*, Billy Charles.

Billy had been a good employer and looked after me well. He had also become a loyal friend in my time there and we had become close. I gave him a number and address he could reach me at if needed, but only in an emergency.

He knew about my gambling debts as he had bailed me out more than once in the past.

He told me if I left London, not to come back in a hurry as Archie Castle wasn't a man not to collect on a debt, especially as big as the one, I owed him. £30,000.

A week later, Ester and I were living in the Harbourside flat in an affluent area of Bristol.

I had certainly gone up in the world.

At first, I missed London and my friends on the doors of the clubs and pubs, but as the weeks went on, things got a little easier.

I once again sorted out employment in clubland and, with my experience, got a vacant head doorman's job at the nightclub *Bubbles* in Bristol city centre. It was a good number in an extremely popular club.

With my new life going well, I had also decided to join Gamblers Anonymous.

My fellow doorman, Ethan Crooks, said that I would never last, and I joked, "You want to bet?"

Ester knew nothing of my gambling debts and that's the way I wanted to keep it.

It is now three months since I have had a bet.

I am still a long way from where I want to be, but I am slowly getting there.

My relationship with Ester is blossoming and in spring of this year we got engaged.

We provisionally pencilled in the following year to get married.

I had never been happier in my life. I had found somebody who loves me for myself, not the boxer and celebrity Eddie Prince.

Although I was happy, the dark spectre of Archie Castle still loomed in the background.

One day whilst I was home alone having a nice nap in a deckchair on the balcony overlooking the Harbourside, my phone pinged in a text.

When I read the caller ID, my stomach lurched. It was Billy Charles. The text read *Call me.*

I immediately rang and was surprised that his wife Tanya answered.

I asked her if everything was okay.

When she answered, her voice was full of fear.

She told me that Archie Castle had paid Billy a visit at his nightclub and asked if he knew my whereabouts as we had been good pals.

Billy denied knowing anything, saying that I had just suddenly disappeared.

Archie wasn't buying it and demanded Billy told him where I was.

Billy kept to the same story until Castle's heavies set about him.

They smashed his kneecaps with lump hammers and were about to start on his elbows when Billy told them.

I asked how Billy was and Tanya said he was recovering in hospital, but it would be a long time before he walked.

I was gutted and gave her my sincere apologies.

She was an East London girl and knew the score. There was no malice towards me.

I then asked her how long ago this incident happened.

Tanya told me two days ago and that Archie Castle would most certainly be coming for me.

As soon as I hung up, I instinctively rang Ester, asking her if she was okay and what time she would be home.

She, in turn, asked if everything was alright and I replied yes, trying to keep the trepidation out of my voice.

My adrenaline was working overtime. I was on code red alert waiting for the inevitable visit. I should have known better that men like Eddie Castle don't just go away.

A day went by but nothing. Then another.

At night whilst Ester slept, I kept a silent vigil at the bedroom window alert to every creak or groan in the flat.

A week went by and still not a word, but I knew he was out there. He was just making me sweat and trying to catch me with my guard down.

I made a story up and told Ester to keep the place locked and secure. I span her some tale that I had heard that burglars were targeting our neighbourhood, I hoped it would be enough to stop her asking any more questions.

I had to keep my work up on the doors. Ester knew I was passionate about it and if I started to stay in on an evening, it would make her suspicious.

Yes, I should have at this point told her, but it had gone too far. She was so in love with me and me her that I didn't want to disappoint her by revealing the truth about my crippling gambling debts.

I couldn't destroy the belief she had in me and the belief she had also installed in myself.

Saturday night, finishing my shift at *Bubbles*, I walked a couple of streets to where I parked my car.

I never parked the car near the club, just in case a disgruntled punter targeted it.

It was 2.00am and the streets were quiet.

As I neared my vehicle, the doors of a black van parked nearby opened and out stepped three guys.

I immediately recognised them as Castle's goons.

I could have run, but I was done with running. This was high noon.

The biggest guy who I knew as 'Fred' told me he had come to collect the debt with interest.

I now owed £50,000 for doing a runner and blanching on the deal I had with Archie.

I told them I didn't have it.

I think they knew that anyway and came at me.

Now I still am a handy boxer, but boxing is a one-on-one sport. It is not ideally designed to take on three, so I had taken to carrying with me a steel extendable baton for extra protection.

As 'Fred' closed in, I took it from my pocket, snapped it open and whipped it hard against his left knee.

Visions of poor old Billy fresh in my mind. Retribution was now on the cards.

I then smashed the baton into the next man's face breaking his nose and teeth with ease.

The last man pulled a knife, but I sent that flying from his hand as I brought the baton down on his wrist bone before backswiping it into his temple.

I looked around just as 'Fred' was getting to his feet.

I ran and brought the baton down on top of his skull sending him face down into the pavement.

I needed to send a message out to these men and Castle not to fuck with me. The message had to be stark and brutal to make Castle stop and think.

The violent side of my nature took over. So, coldly, I moved around the bodies breaking elbows and knees with the baton.

I told them to tell Archie if he had the balls to come looking for me, he would get the same. So, fuck him and his money.

Once finished and breathing heavily, I walked across the road to my car. I checked to see if there was anybody around, but all was quiet apart from the loud beating of my heart.

I took comfort in the fact that this quiet side street had no CCTV cameras.

By my car was a drain. I slipped the baton through the grating and into the sewer below.

As I started my car, I glanced at the fallen bodies. They lay still.

I drove away.

Halfway home, my mobile phone rang. I saw it was Ester calling and answered it immediately.

She told me that somebody had rang the flat's intercom on more than one occasion but had said nothing. She went on to say she thought that somebody was outside in the carpark watching the flat.

I told her to stay put and I would be back in ten minutes.

I put my foot down now worried for Ester.

As I pulled into the car park, I scanned the area. Suddenly, a parked car's headlights came on and a vehicle pulled away at speed. I watched it go.

I suspected it was Castle. He knew from Billy where I lived.

Once in the flat, I comforted Ester and told her I had seen nothing untoward.

That night I lay in bed wondering whether the carnage I left would make Castle back off or whether it would make him more determined. I hoped and prayed it wouldn't be the latter.

To make sure Ester was safe, I persuaded her to go and visit her mother for a few days as she had mentioned she was considering this recently. She agreed.

Knowing she would be in Surrey and miles away from here made me feel more comfortable.

That evening, whilst on the door, she rang me. I asked if she was okay and she told me she was fine, but had some news for me. She said she was four weeks pregnant and that I was going to be a dad. I was over the moon and couldn't wait to tell the lads on the door.

But she told me to keep it under my hat until she had been to the clinic for her ten-week check.

Reluctantly, I agreed, but I was one happy man.

A few months passed and there was no more sign of Castle or his thugs.

It looked like my message had done the trick.

With a new baby on the way and me not having gambled for months, life seemed to be on the turn at last for Eddie Prince.

CHAPTER THREE

It was Saturday 22nd December 2018, three days before Christmas. People were out and about celebrating the festive season. The pubs and clubs in Bristol were heaving.

It wasn't going to be a white Christmas, according to the experts. At the moment, it was surprisingly mild with a drizzle in the air, but it didn't dampen the spirits of the late-night revellers in the city centre.

Eddie Prince stood on the door of *Bubbles* nightclub along with fellow doorman Ethan Crooks.

The club inside was full and everybody seemed to be in a Christmassy mood. There hadn't been any trouble of note this evening.

Eddie and Ethan had an hour left of their shift.

Eddie was looking forward to getting home to Ester.

She was due to give birth in the next week or so. It was to be a special Christmas for them.

Eddie was looking forward to becoming a father.

He had become a changed man over the last six months.

Gambling was now something in the past.

He was also considering coming off the doors in the new year.

Well, it wasn't the best of jobs for prospective parenthood.

They had also recently moved out of the one-bedroom flat into a beautiful detached four-bedroom house.

The nursery was decorated in pinks and blues and ready for their new arrival.

With Ester's help and encouragement, Eddie had embarked on an open college network degree in business studies. If he successfully passed it, he was considering opening a boxing-themed restaurant.

It was exciting times. Eddie's life had totally changed for the better since he first met his beautiful lady.

Eddie now regarded Ethan Crooks stood next to him. He had become a reliable ally on the door. Crooks had been a professional Thai boxer and had proved his ability many a time in front of Eddie.

There was 14 stone of chiselled black muscle under his suit and Eddie trusted him with his life.

They made a formidable team.

'So, what are your plans for Christmas, my friend?' asked Eddie.

Ethan's face broke into a big smile.

'Well, Christmas day will be at my family's house. Mum always expects me to be there.'

Eddie knew Ethan had four siblings and that they were a tight family.

'Then, Boxing Day, I will take a little drive over to Bath for some Christmas loving with the adorable Gemma.'

Eddie nodded.

'Sounds like you are sorted.'

'I bet you and your lady are having a quiet Christmas waiting on the arrival of the little one, I suspect,' asked Ethan.

'You got it right there. Christmas can't come fast enough for me. Next year is going to be a good one,' replied Eddie.

Ethan high-fived him.

'Amen to that, brother, and on that note, I have to take a quick piss. I won't be a moment.'

'No worries. I am fine here.'

Once Ethan had disappeared into the club, Eddie walked down a couple of the front steps of the club and looked up and down the road.

Although it was gone 1.00am, the place was nearly still as busy as it was on a Saturday afternoon.

People were milling around the takeaway shops or lining up in the taxi ranks.

'I must be getting old,' he mused as all he needed now was his bed.

Just then a BMW pulled up to the kerb and the driver's window slid down.

A stunning black girl looked out of the window at him.

'Excuse me, handsome. I am looking for Berkeley Square. Am I anywhere near it?'

Eddie smiled.

'Yes. If you go back around the one-way system and bear off to the left, you will come right into it.'

The black girl's face now split into a beautiful smile.

'Thank you, my sat nav has gone on the blink and I got a little lost. You are a lifesaver.'

'My pleasure,' replied Eddie.

The girl eyed him coolly.

'Are you Eddie Prince, the boxer?'

Eddie was surprised that a girl so young would recognise him.

'Yes, I am.'

'I thought so. My name is Georgia. My daddy was a boxer, and I was brought up on the sport. I have seen footage of your world title fight in Vegas on YouTube.'

'Well, that's nice to know. What is your dad's name? I might know of him.'

'His name was Errol Wallace. Welterweight in the 1990s.

'Can't say I recall the name,' answered Eddie.

'I have a picture here of him in my bag. Check it out if you like.'

Eddie walked up to the car as the girl produced a photograph for him to look at.

Just then, the rear window silently opened and the ominous shape of a Glock 17 with a large suppressor on the barrel pointed out at Eddie who was engrossed with looking at the photo.

Eddie then heard a familiar voice.

'Should have paid me my money, Eddie. I always collect a debt in the end, no matter how long I have to wait.'

As Eddie turned towards the source of the voice, a bullet hit him squarely between the eyes.

He hadn't stood a chance from such close proximity. He was dead before he hit the pavement.

Ethan Crooks had come out of the front door of the club just at the moment the horrific event occurred.

The Black BMW had sped away into the night.

Eddie Prince lay lifeless on the pavement as a crowd started to gather around.

CHAPTER FOUR

Simon

I have survived the operation. I feel like I have been run over by a truck, but I am alive. I have been informed that the transplant seems to have been a success.

I am so glad to be alive and have another chance at life.

I have never been a particularly religious man, but I have prayed every day up to and since the operation to God and gave thanks.

I know I am fortunate.

A donor match had come relatively quickly.

I had been sat on my sofa on a wet Thursday lunch time watching *Loose Woman* engrossed in the subject matter about where a female's G spot is.

It was compelling TV as I didn't even know were A, B, C, D, E and F were, let alone G.

Was it like playing the notes on a musical instrument?

I was just about to spoon the first mouthful of delicious Scandinavian low-fat natural yoghurt into my mouth when my mobile phone had sounded.

It was my heart transplant co-ordinator. A lovely nurse by the name of Aadya Shamar.

She informed me that they had found a match and I was to come straight in for the procedure.

I was booked into the Royal Brompton Hospital in Chelsea, West London.

Royal Brompton had a 170-year history of heart and lung transplants.

It boasted over 2,200 staff.

I was going to be in good hands.

I had been fortunate that it was just over five months of waiting. I was lucky as many people waited years living a life in what can only be described as suspended animation.

Aadya had been marvellous from the first day I met her.

I had gone through many vigorous and thorough tests to get to this stage.

Blood tests, X-rays, BP tests, CT and MRI scans, ultrasounds, angiograms, ECGs.

You name it, I had it.

But, before you can be placed on the transplant list, you must go through a careful screening process. A team of heart doctors, nurses, social workers, and bioethicists review your medical history, diagnostic test results, social history and psychological test results to see if you are able to survive the procedure and then comply with the continuous care needed to live a healthy life.

I had been in hospital more times than George Clooney in the whole series of ER.

The right heart size and blood group were vital in the process.

My group was O. Apparently, 48% of the UK population have O blood group. That made it a little easier to find a match.

I began to research heart transplants. I wanted to know as much as I could on the subject. It made me feel more prepared.

The first-ever successful heart transplant operation was performed in South Africa in 1967 by Prof. Christiaan Neethling Barnard and a team of 30 physicians at the Groote Schuur Hospital, Cape Town. The patient, Louis Washkansky, survived for 18 days with the new heart.

The first ever heart transplant in the UK was performed on 3rd May 1968 by a surgeon named Donald Ross. The patient only lasted 45 days. 1979 was the first successful transplant in the UK. It was performed by Sir Terence English at the famous Papworth hospital in Cambridgeshire.

2019 saw Royal Papworth perform to date 1,887 heart transplants.

8,400 since the first one in 1968.

Over 50,000 people worldwide have received new hearts.

What an incredible achievement. You would never think of this until you are in my situation.

I am under no illusions that 75% of successful heart transplant patients only live five years.

Some between five and ten years.

Although a John McCafferty, who had a transplant in 1982 at the age of 39, only recently passed away in 2016 at the age of 73. Amazing.

At present, in the Guinness Book of Records, a man in Iowa, U.S.A is still living after 34 years.

I would love to be that guy, but he is definitely the exception to the rule.

Personally, I am grateful to get a second chance to embrace another sunrise and, for however long that may be, the old Simon Winter is dead.

I had changed my ways and hoped to continue doing so.

Before going in for this operation, I had lost over two stone simply by cutting out junk food and walking every day. I was determined to carry this on once I recovered.

The recipient of the donor's heart can only be told the following things.

The donor's age, gender, type of death.

You are not told name, occupation or D.O.B.

The donor's family will only know the recipient's age range, gender and outcome of the transplant.

When I went into hospital and received the information about the donor, I was in for a shock.

Aadya had previously told me there were limited things she could tell me.

She told me the donor had been 45 years old at death. The donor had been a very fit male, so the heart was extremely healthy. He had coincidently lived locally.

My black humour kicked in and I said he couldn't have been that fit if he was dead at 45.

This is when I got the shock: Aadya told me he had been the victim of a shooting.

That piece of news wiped the smile off of my face, I can tell you.

Aadya went on to say she could understand if this freaked me out and if I wanted, I could wait for another match if I was uncomfortable.

I must admit it did feel strange to be having the heart of a person who had been shot dead, but I may have had to wait years for another perfect match to come around again, so I told her to go ahead with it.

As I said, it all went well. The operation took five hours and 34 seconds, according to the surgeon Sir Alex Fordham. This was his 40th transplant operation. I didn't have the balls to ask what percentage of them had been successful.

I am constantly monitored, but everything seems to be working as it should.

I will be on immunosuppressants for the rest of my days, so my body doesn't reject the heart or get an infection.

Doctors will frequently do a biopsy to take small pieces of the new heart to examine.

This is done weekly for the first three to six weeks after surgery. Then every three months for a year. Then once a year.

I will start cardiac rehabilitation as soon as I leave hospital. If I keep on improving, I will be released from hospital in two to three weeks' time.

If all goes well, it will be 6-12 weeks before any strenuous exercise or sex.

The sex thing won't be too much of a problem as I have gone a considerably longer time without it already.

I will hopefully be able to drive around 12 weeks.

Exercise will be gradual as the nerve endings of my new heart beat faster (100 to 110 bpm) than the normal heart (70 to 80 bpm).

I now have no excuse not to exercise and address my diet.

If I don't, then I won't be around long.

So, a new Simon Winter is coming home.

He hopes to be a better Simon Winter and a braver one.

A Simon Winter who stops being afraid of his own shadow and lives life to the full.

We will see.

CHAPTER FIVE

6 months later

The heart transplant had been a success and Simon had turned his whole life around.

The first 12 weeks were tough. The rehabilitation was not easy, but Simon surprised himself by really working hard with a determination he didn't know he had in him.

At the end of rehab, the cardiac team were pleased with his results and encouraged him to keep the steady and gradual training going.

Simon promised he would, but unlike other times he had said this to doctors, this time inside he knew he meant it.

The cardiac rehab had been held weekly in a local sports centre gym and Simon was surprised how he had taken to it. His fear of gyms seemed to be totally unwarranted.

Since he had left hospital, he had made steady progress each month.

When Simon had his cardiac arrest, he weighed 18 stone. He now weighed 14.

He had walked and swam regularly and had recently begun to jog.

It was early days for this, but he was doing it.

He had never imagined in his life that he would be jogging around his local park.

Simon had also stuck to his clean eating habits.

He allowed himself the odd weekly treat, but in general, his junk food binges were in the past.

He looked and felt better for it.

New bathroom scales had been purchased not only recording weight but also BMI, body fat and body composition.

Simon could again look at himself in a full-length mirror and not be repulsed.

He felt rejuvenated and happy.

His new lifestyle opened all sorts of possibilities for him.

He had a new job based in Bristol employed as branch manager for estate agents *Property Plus*.

He had left his old company wanting to cut down on his driving time to and from Wales so that old habits and temptations wouldn't resurface again.

He was now dealing in a particular area of Bristol which required minimal time in a car.

It suited him perfectly, plus his employees were glad to take on a man with his experience.

Jean and the kids had been in touch regularly and when he had popped around the house to take the kids out for the day, he couldn't fail to see how impressed his wife was with the new Simon.

Slimmer and fitter sporting a designer haircut and beard.

His clothes were a few sizes smaller, fitting nicely.

Crisp blue shirt, beige chinos and a pair of brown Timberland boots.

The beer belly and double chin were gone, so were the bloodshot eyes and bad teeth.

Simon Winter had received the full makeover and things were looking up.

Jean had to admit her ex-husband was looking hot.

She never thought that she would ever be thinking this.

Simon himself began to feel attractive again which, in turn, boosted his confidence in many areas of his life.

At his local leisure centre, he could use the gym, but was still under the supervision of a cardiac rehab personal trainer.

A regular gym user had caught his eye. A rather stunning blonde lady.

In Simon's old life, she would have been out of his league and probably wouldn't have given him a second glance.

She was in her late thirties, with an incredible figure that was honed daily with exercise.

It had all started with a nod and a smile as they seemed to always be in the gym at the same time. Then it became 'hello', before going on to first name terms and then eventually a bit of flirting.

Her name was Andrea Golding.

Simon had found out she wasn't married, and he made sure that she knew he was separated.

She wasn't just a looker. He found out Andrea was a smart cookie and worked as a senior member of the cabin crew for B.A.

One evening they had walked out of the leisure centre at the same moment and Simon found himself asking Andrea if she would like to go for a drink with him at the local pub down the road, The Queen's Shilling.

He was amazed when she said she would love to.

In the pub they found a quiet table to sit at. Simon asked Andrea what she would like to drink.

'I would love a G&T, please.'

As she said this, she crossed her legs and Simon couldn't fail to see her tight mini skirt ride up displaying a shapely thigh.

Simon walked to the bar with a stirring in his loins. He had not felt that for a long time, and he liked it.

At the bar, he order the G&T and got a glass of soda water and lime for himself.

This was not part of his health plan, but strangely, since the transplant, he had gone right off all alcohol.

He couldn't understand it since he had been in pubs and drank since a 16-year-old kid.

A few weeks back, he had a glass of his favourite red wine with his dinner, and he had been violently sick later.

Alcohol just didn't taste the same anymore.

He had asked Aadya if this might be down to the medication he was on, and she informed him that it could be, although others who had undergone the same operation could drink alcohol in moderation with no ill effects.

Simon didn't miss alcohol. He also didn't miss his 20-a-day habit or his love for McDonalds.

Strangely, he had no cravings for any junk food.

In general, he was so much healthier. His heart had not given him any problems and he was beginning to exercise more and more with no ill effects.

Occasionally, he noticed for no reason he would get a sharp and painful headache that would last a short while and then just disappear. Also, at night sometimes, he found he would wake up suddenly from a nightmare and feel scared. He couldn't recall exactly what he dreamt about, but the fear stayed with him for a while.

It could be unsettling and many times he would get up and sit in the living room with all the lights on and the television until the feelings subsided.

He reasoned if that were all the problems he had after all he had been through, then he could live with it.

The cardiac team told him he may find some changes after the transplant.

Some people find God or see life differently. Their priorities change. Others may have to deal with various medical side effects for the rest of their lives.

So far, any changes Simon felt seemed to be for the better.

Simon brought the drinks back to the table and sat down.

Andrea and he talked like they had known each other all their lives.

Simon couldn't believe he felt so comfortable and confident with this woman.

He had always felt a little awkward in female company, although most of the time, he could have been invisible as most woman never gave him a second glance.

Well, things were different here.

Andrea was giving out strong signals that she more than fancied him.

It had been a long time since Simon had felt wanted.

Things were going along nicely until when Simon stood up to get some more drinks, he inadvertently pushed back his chair as a man was going past behind him.

The chair knocked into the man causing him to spill some of his pint over the floor.

'Fucking hell, you numpty. Look what you've done!' exclaimed the man in an angry tone.

Simon was immediately apologetic.

'Shit, I am sorry, mate. I didn't see you there.'

The man was obviously agitated by what happened and by the glazed expression in his eyes he had had a few.

'Are you fucking blind or what?' he asked aggressively getting right up in Simon's face.

Simon regarded the man.

He estimated that he was in his middle thirties. He was big. He looked like he worked out with weights. He had a tattoo of a dragon on his right bicep.

The man was posturing puffing out his chest and splaying his arms.

'I asked you a fucking question, pal. Are you fucking blind or what?'

Andrea was feeling extremely uncomfortable and fearing somewhat for Simon.

Simon knew where this was heading. He hated confrontation. He had spent the best part of his life running away from it.

Fighting and violence weren't his thing. He had a thing about blood, especially if it was his.

He tried to keep the tremor out of his voice when he answered.

'No, I am not blind. I just didn't see you there that's all. Can I get you another drink?'

The man's face was bright red as he snarled.

'I don't want another fucking drink. How about you wipe the spilled beer off of my new trainers instead? They cost me a fortunate and you have just ruined them.'

The incident was now drawing attention.

The barman called over from behind the bar.

'Everything okay there, Keith?'

His voice showed concern.

Without taking his eyes off of Simon, the man called Keith answered back.

'Everything is fine, John. You carry on, me and my new friend here are just sorting out a little disagreement.'

The barman, John, didn't look convinced.

'I don't want any trouble in here, Keith.'

Keith smiled.

'No worries, John. We are just sorting this out now.'

He looked back at Simon.

'Well, go get some bog paper and clean my shoes and then we are done.'

The man looked in Andrea's direction.

'Then you can go back to talking to this gorgeous babe.'

As he said this his eyes roamed lecherously over Andrea's body.

Simon felt sick to the stomach.

He looked Keith in the eye and said, 'I am not going to do that. I offered a drink, which you refused, so that is it as far as I am concerned.'

Simon looked to Andrea.

He saw fear in her eyes.

'Come on. We are leaving.'

Keith put his pint down on the table and stood in front of Simon.

'You aren't going anywhere, asshole.'

Simon felt his legs turn to jelly.

His heart was pounding in his chest. He didn't like this feeling.

It brought him back to his schooldays and the procession of bullies that had tormented him.

Simon remembered 'Ginger Phil'. A bully. School rugby player and all-round asshole.

He had made his life a misery.

One particular incident was burnt into Simon's memory banks.

'Ginger Phil' and his cronies had cornered Simon up on the playing fields of the school and searched him taking a couple of pounds off him, which was Simon's bus fare home.

Simon pleaded to have the money back as he needed to get home on time as his parents were going out of a meal to celebrate their wedding anniversary.

'Ginger Phil' told Simon if he licked his shoes, he would give him the money back.

Simon protested, but 'Ginger Phil' said it was that or he walked away with his money.

Simon didn't want to ruin his parents evening, so he got down on his knees and licked 'Ginger Phil's' shoes.

The gang all laughed and walked off with his money anyway.

Simon was so angry and frustrated that he had degraded himself for nothing.

He walked home and was late and received a bollocking from his father telling him how irresponsible he was and how they would be late for the restaurant.

Simon never told his parents why he was late. He just bottled it up and loathed himself more than ever.

He took comfort in a tub of chocolate ice cream in the freezer instead.

Simon now breathed deeply and went to move past the man, but Keith put his hand on his chest and blocked his way.

'Stay the fuck where you are, or you'll get a slap.'

Simon's breathing quickened and his heart thumped in his chest.

He was transported back to school and the man in front of him morphed into 'Ginger Phil'.

What happened next Simon could not explain. He could only describe it later as an out of body experience.

He brushed the man's hand away and hit him with a solid right hook on the jawbone.

It was a perfect connection. Bone on bone.

As Keith staggered back with eyes rolling in his head, Simon was on him like a panther.

The first punch was followed up by a vicious left hook to the liver, right uppercut to the chin and another left hook to the head.

The man named Keith crashed back into the table behind him and sunk to the floor unconscious.

Simon moved forward and grabbed a handful of Keith's t-shirt and looked into the bleeding man's features.

Although the man was out of it, Simon hoped his voice would penetrate through his subconscious.

When he spoke, Simon didn't recognise the venom and power in his voice.

'Not so fucking tough now, are you, prick? Don't ever fuck with me again, you piece of shit, or I will kill you.'

Simon shoved the unconscious man back to the floor.

He looked around the bar with wild eyes. Adrenaline was coursing around his body like a speeding bullet.

'Anybody else want some? Well, do you?'

The room was silent.

Obviously, nobody had ever done this to Keith before. The clientele were in shock.

Andrea stared open-mouthed at Simon.

She too couldn't believe what had just happened.

The most surprised person in the place though was Simon.

The fog in his head seemed to lift.

His heart rate began to decrease with no ill effects.

It had been like watching the whole scenario through another person's eyes.

He gave Andrea a weak smile.

'Come on. Let's go.'

Nobody stood in his way as they left.

At the door, Simon stopped and looked across to John the barman and said, 'You better phone Keith there an ambulance.'

Outside, as they walked back to Simon's car, Andrea couldn't contain her excitement.

'Jesus, Simon, were you a boxer at some time in your life? You never said. You were like Muhammad Ali. That bully never knew what hit him. Are you okay? I mean, after your transplant and all that. Shit, it's unbelievable. I am dating the bloody Terminator.'

Simon didn't know what to say. He was still in shock himself.

He had never hit another person in his life, yet a few moments ago, he did it like a pro.

Andrea seemed mighty impressed.

She linked his arm and snuggled into his shoulder as they walked along.

As soon as they had entered Andrea's flat and shut the door, she was on him like a wild animal.

She pinned him to the wall and found his lips.

Between passionate kisses, she told him how the whole thing had turned her on and she wanted him here and now.

Simon found himself responding.

He was growing hard, which was not a usual occurrence.

Again, Simon felt a strange sensation come over him.

He didn't know what the hell was happening to him, but he liked it.

They ripped at their clothes as their hands roamed over each other's bodies.

Simon grabbed Andrea and lifted her into his arms and carried her to the kitchen where he lay her down on the dining table ripping her underwear away.

He was ready and immediately thrusted into her.

The lovemaking was fast and frenzied and soon over.

But they then retired to the bedroom where they made love again, this time more controlled and slower.

Simon savoured every inch of Andrea's incredible body.

It had been so long since he had a woman that he thought he might be dreaming, but no, this was real.

The next morning, they made love again, this time in the shower.

Simon felt rejuvenated. He was like a horny teenager.

He never thought he would have these intense feelings ever again.

When he had recovered from the heart transplant, he didn't know what level of living he would have, but never in his wildest dreams did he think he would be doing this.

Seemingly overnight, he had become a fighter and a lover all rolled into one.

What the hell had happened to Simon Winter?

CHAPTER SIX

Simon

It is a month since the incident in the pub. I have thought about it incessantly.

I still have no idea how I did what I did.

All my life I had been a bit of a coward and, as I have mentioned before, avoided any violence like the plague.

I have never had a boxing lesson in my life or indeed been remotely interested in the sport.

I could never see the point in two grown men punching each other in the head for money.

Yet in that pub I had hit that bullying prick Keith with punches that suggested I was a veteran of the square ring.

The man had been big and scary, yet I had felt no fear.

I feel a bit like one of those Marvel comic book characters, Peter Parker or Bruce Banner, who suddenly discovered they had hidden superpowers.

This frightens me, but also exhilarates me at the same time.

It still exhilarates Andrea and things, shall we say, are still smouldering.

She can't keep her hands off me and I am not complaining.

Since my loveless marriage ended, I never thought that I would have another woman be interested in me. I almost resigned myself to that fact.

Well, let's face it, at the time I wasn't exactly what you might call a catch.

But since I lost weight and started taking pride in my appearance, my luck has certainly changed.

Andrea is amazing in bed. More than I could have dreamt for. I am a lucky man.

Sometimes I get worried that the old ticker might give up when we are rolling around in the sheets.

But here's the thing. I have also been getting attention from another couple of women.

Firstly, there is Carol, and she works on the checkout of my local Asda. We have struck up a nice little friendship. We have a bit of saucy banter together whenever I shop there.

She is married, but she is flirting with me more and more. I am thinking of asking her out. Well, just because I can.

The other woman is Eve, and she has recently moved in the same flats as I live in. I have bumped into her on a few occasions.

She is single and lives with her cocker spaniel Timmy.

I am not a great animal lover, but I have pretended I am. She likes this.

The other evening, she knocked on my door and asked if I could come take a look at her television as it wasn't working.

I changed a fuse in the plug, and all was good.

I stayed for a coffee, and I got the distinct feeling we have a spark between us.

Eve asked me if I would like to come around for dinner Saturday night.

Well, how could I refuse? I am a man reborn, and the opposite sex suddenly find me attractive.

Amazing, since I used to be the sort of guy who looked at the sell-by date on a packet of Durex and wondered if I would ever use them by then.

I suppose it is wrong to string Andrea along, but what she doesn't know won't hurt her.

Andrea's job meant she was away for days on end, which made things handy if you were seeing other women.

I am not interested in any long-term relationship. After all, I don't know how long I have got on this planet, and I don't really want anything heavy. I want to seize the moment and enjoy my time.

The transplant guaranteed nothing. It certainly is another shot at life, but you never know when the old ticker says, 'fuck you' and decides to pack up.

You just have to live from week to week and not make too many long-term plans.

Jean and I have started the process of divorce which, again, I had been procrastinating about for a year or more.

She wants to marry Tommy and I am cool with that.

I just want a nice clean break from memories of my old life.

As long as I have access to the kids, then that is fine.

So, I have decided to make the most of the opportunities coming my way.

The old Simon would never have done this.

I have lost more weight and I have become a gym rat. Who would have thought it?

I am in there most evenings after work and weekends.

Little old me who hated exercise and wouldn't be seen dead in a gym for fear of making a fool of himself.

Now I am well known in there and on first name terms with a lot of the staff and other gym users.

I can't quite get my head around it.

I am totally relaxed in that environment as if I am meant to be there.

It's like I have had a personality bypass.

But as I see myself transforming in the mirror, the training is like a drug urging me on to find out just how far I can go.

Yesterday I began to notice the outline of a six pack. Amazing as before the operation the only six pack I was familiar with was the Stella Artois in my fridge.

The scar on my chest has healed well to a pale pink hue.

I have taken up getting a spray tan whenever needed and that hides it even more.

Fucking spray tans. What is wrong with me?

I always used to berate the spray tan brigade. Now I could give David Dickinson a run for his money.

I still get the headaches now and again and the nightmares.

I have grown to live with them for now.

My medical check-ups have been fine.

The heart seems to be coping well enough, and I have made more progress than expected.

As I mentioned, the weight is coming off nicely. My BMI is now in normal range and my body fat is around 20%, which is a healthy range for my age.

The other day I was in town and passed a department store shop window and I saw my reflection. I wondered for a moment who it was staring back at me.

For so long I was that fat man and now it is sometimes hard to belief I am not.

Remember my best mate, Greg Badcock? Yes, he is still a fat bastard and no longer speaks to me as we now have nothing in common.

I realised our common bond had been alcohol and kebabs. Beyond that not much more, except we had both been separated from our wives.

So, most Saturday nights in the pub followed the same pathway.

It had been drinks a plenty until we reached a maudlin point in the evening where we then started on the whisky feeling sorry for ourselves and then finally both go and find solace at the nearest kebab shop.

Not anymore though.

Greg called me a sanctimonious prick when I tried to enthuse to him about the benefits of fitness and healthy eating. He wasn't interested and I knew we had grown apart.

He told me that I wouldn't keep this new regime up and in six months' time I would be back to my old habits.

It was bravado on his part. He could see his old friend had well and truly gone. He just hadn't come to terms with it yet.

Many people find change hard to deal with, whether it be in their own life or with somebody close to them.

It unnerves them. They don't like being taken out of their comfort zone.

I remember the old saying.

'Ships are safe in dock, but ships are made to sail.'

When some people close to the person sees them begin to grow and change, it frightens them so they will bring as much negativity as they can down on them in the hope they will stay where they are.

The successful people in this world constantly break out of their comfort zones for horizons new and if that means leaving so-called friends behind so be it.

If they were true friends, they would be encouraging you and wishing you luck.

The last time I met Greg in a pub, he tried to get me to have a few beers for old times' sake, but I wasn't interested. I told him I would happily sit down with him for a while, but I was alright with my soda water and lime.

He couldn't handle it and called me a 'Gay boy.'

It was a stupid childish comment.

We argued and it ended with him telling me to fuck off, which I did.

That was it. The friendship done.

I was sad but knew we were now poles apart, it was nobody's fault. Maybe I had pushed him too hard to change his ways? Who the fuck was I to preach?

If I hadn't had the heart attack, I would most likely still be sat there with him necking down the beers and gorging on pork scratchings.

But I couldn't help feeling that I had to tell everybody I knew about my complete turn around and how well I felt and all the benefits that it brought.

At first they were all over the moon for me, but over a period of time, I suspect I began to sound like a broken record. Many disappeared into the night.

I was gradually building a new circle of like-minded friends though and they looked up to me as their mentor, so to speak. How had I developed such confidence and self-belief when most of my life I had been fearful of everything and anything?

The very last time I saw Greg was by chance. I was on a bus, and it pulled up at a stop in town right outside McDonalds and there he was sat at the window wolfing down a Big Mac.

As the bus pulled in, he looked up and our eyes meet momentarily. He then turned away and took another bite from his burger totally blanking me.

This saddened me. We went back a long way. It was a pity our relationship had ended like this.

But I was now on a different journey, and it wasn't one where the Greg Badcocks of the world would be travelling.

By the way, two weeks ago I learnt from a friend of his that Greg had keeled over and died from a heart attack in his favourite pub, the Golden Lion, whilst singing karaoke.

Ironically, he had been in the middle of singing Queen's *Another One Bites the Dust*.

I attended the funeral and kept myself lowkey. I declined the offer to go back to the house for the wake.

Greg had been 42 years of age, the same age as me when I had my heart attack. The only difference was Greg wasn't given another chance.

CHAPTER SEVEN

Simon woke up from a nightmare with a start and sat bolt upright in his bed. He glanced at the bedside clock. It read 3.30am.

He had one of his headaches again. The pain was right between his eyes. He knew he would need some paracetamol to help ease it.

Simon threw back the duvet carefully not wanting to wake Eve and went to the bathroom where he had seen some tablets in the wall cabinet earlier on.

He pressed two out of their foil blister pack and swilled them down with a handful of tap water.

He regarded himself in the mirror.

This nightmare had been more vivid than the others. He had seen the features of a man, but had no idea who it was. His face had been noticeably clear, and he looked angry.

Simon sucked in another handful of water. The wispy remnants of the nightmare were now fading to the corners of his mind.

He moved back into the bedroom and sat on an easy chair by the window.

He was in Eve's flat, and he had taken up her invitation for dinner, which had been lovely. The 'afters' had been even better. Totally unexpected but very welcoming. Eve was a little minx and certainly knew how to please a man in bed.

He had been exhausted when he finally drifted off to sleep around 1.00am.

Suddenly, a noise caught his attention.

He looked to the open bedroom door and Timmy the cocker spaniel padded in.

The dog came up to Simon and jumped up onto his lap.

Simon softly stroked the dog and found it calming. His headache began to ease.

He wondered why now the headaches usually only occurred before the nightmares and not at any other time. Was there a connection?

Eve murmured in her sleep and rolled over onto her side.

Simon went back to his thoughts.

Earlier that day, he had experienced another incident that unnerved him.

He had been driving home to his flat.

In front of him was a cyclist. A young woman.

As she passed a side turning, a car drove straight out without looking and knocked her clean off her bike with a sickening crunch.

Simon had to perform an emergency stop so as not to run over her.

As he got out of his car to help the woman, to his amazement, the car that had hit her, a blue Renault, tried to drive away but stalled its engine.

Simon stared incredulously at the man in the car as he jumped out of the driver's seat and started running up the street.

Simon had the overwhelming desire to give chase, but he had to see to the woman who was lying still on the road.

He approached her and saw her left leg badly buckled. There was an open fracture of the lower leg with the bone exposed.

Her face was also bloodied from a head wound, which had knocked her unconscious.

Simon knelt and surveyed her for any more injuries.

He knew he should turn her onto her side to aid her breathing and prevent her choking, but he wasn't sure if she had any spinal injuries.

Thankfully, he had the decision taken away from him as another bystander had already phoned an ambulance that was on the way.

Simon stayed with the woman until the paramedics arrived and took over.

He then gave an account of what had happened to the police and a good description of the man that had fled the scene.

It was only when he returned to his car that he realised how composed he had been and that the blood and injury to the woman hadn't freaked him out at all.

This was amazing as he had a diagnosed phobia of blood since a child and had never got over it until now that is.

The police had rung him some time later to tell him that the woman had regained consciousness and was comfortable in hospital.

They also informed him that they had found the man in the blue Renault. The car had been stolen and he was found in a local park smoking pot. He was high as a kite.

He was now in police custody.

Simon was suddenly roused from his thoughts.

'Hi, Mister, are you coming back to bed? It's cold in here without you.'

He smiled at Eve.

'I am on my way, your ladyship.'

Simon slipped back under the covers and spooned up against Eve's naked body.

'Are you okay, Simon?' she asked.

'Yeah. I am fine. Just find it difficult sometimes to sleep. That's all.

Eve turned around to face him and her hand strayed down his body.

'Well, if you are awake, Buster, maybe you should make use of the time. What do you think?'

Simon smiled in the darkness and answered.

'Why not.'

CHAPTER EIGHT

Simon

I am now jogging regularly in the park, and I am able to run 3 km, which I am extremely proud of.

I sometimes take Timmy with me for company. Occasionally, Eve also comes.

I am having a problem on the women front as both Eve and Andrea want me to move in with them.

I like them both, but I have told them I need my independence.

I stressed to them that I was coming out of a tough marriage and overcoming a major surgery.

I needed to find my own way and maintain my own space.

They both bought it for now and, to be honest, it was partially true.

The other truth was I didn't want to move in with either of them.

I was too busy playing the field and the field had got bigger as last Friday I had taken the delectable Carol from Asda out for a drink, and we got on like a house on fire.

She had been separated from a very controlling and violent husband for over a year.

She had custody of her two children and there was a restraining order on her old man.

Carol was making a new life for herself, and I admired her for that.

We chose a restaurant out of town away from prying eyes and got a taxi there and back.

When the taxi dropped us back at her house, she asked if I wanted to come in for a coffee.

I would have loved to, but I found myself declining her offer telling her I had to get up early for work, which was a lie, but it just didn't feel right to take up her invitation. Not just yet.

I knew what coffee would lead to and although I was enjoying my new role as a Don Juan, I felt this woman was still vulnerable and fragile.

I didn't want to push things until I knew what it was that I wanted from all the female company in my life at present.

I had gone from having to content myself with watching late night adult channels to now fighting off gorgeous ladies from all corners.

As I walked home that night, it was the first time that I seriously analysed my life since the transplant.

It had been a rollercoaster.

Instead of the transplant impeding my life, it had done the opposite; it had turned it on its head.

I really don't recognise myself. Not just physically, but psychologically.

The old Simon Winter was fading away in front of my eyes.

I now kicked out faster as I ran towards the lake in the park. The crisp morning air felt good in my lungs. I could feel my heart beating steadily in my chest. I never thought I would enjoy running so much.

Suddenly, a thought occurred to me. As a long-term goal, wouldn't it be crazy if I ran a marathon?

That would wipe the smile off my ex-wife's face and her 'running man' Tommy Norris.

As I continued to run, the plan formulated.

I could do it for the British Heart Foundation and raise money and awareness for the cause.

Maybe get the TV and newspapers to get involved.

A heart transplant patient running a fucking marathon. Now that would be something.

It's feasible.

I have gone online and read about the amazing feats of people who had heart transplants.

There have been numerous reports in both the popular media and in the medical literature of people who are able to perform at an impressive level of physical fitness post-heart transplant.

From competitive cycling, gruelling endurance competitions, climbing the world's tallest peaks and participation in the national and international Transplant Games, some transplant recipients are able to achieve a level of physical fitness that allows them to participate in competitive athletic events.

It is also possible that as future studies better elucidate the most effective intensity, duration and timing of exercise training post-transplantation that a greater number of patients may be able to participate in competitive athletics than previously thought possible.

The more I thought about the idea the more I warmed to it.

By the time I was walking back towards the park gates, I was totally sold on the idea.

Then a black cloud appeared, intent on ruining my day.

As I neared the gate, a white van pulled up outside.

On the side of it, red lettering announced G.P. Plumbing and Heating.

A man got out of the driver's side.

He was mid-forties, stocky build and bald as a snooker ball. He had a familiar look of menace about him.

He came towards me.

'Are you Simon Winter?' he asked aggressively.

I became wary of him.

I didn't know him, but he knew my name.

'Yes. Why?' I replied.

The man screwed his face up in anger.

'I will tell you why, pal. I heard you have been getting cosy with my missus.'

I didn't like where this was heading, especially as another tough looking man got out the passenger side of the van and joined us.

I had to think on my feet.

'I don't know what you mean. You must have the wrong person.'

The man turned to the other one that had joined him and asked.

'Is this the joker that was in your taxicab last Friday with Carol?'

The man answered.

'That's him alright, Gary. Picked them up from your old house, took them to the Red Moon restaurant on the Clevedon Road and then picked them back up and dropped them back off at yours again.'

The bald man smiled.

'I am Gary Pickering, Carol's husband. Jimmy here works as a labourer for my plumbing firm and then does a bit of taxi work at weekends. What a coincidence he picked you up. He clocked the address straight away and then later told me. I paid Carol a little visit to find out more about you and she gave up the information after a little persuasion and here I am catching you on your early morning run.'

The mention of him visiting Carol made my stomach churn.

'You better not have hurt her, you bastard.'

A sickly grin spread over the man's face.

'That's my business pal. I am here to tell you to back off and leave her alone. She belongs to me. Always has, always will. Understand?'

I now felt my blood boil.

'I understand that you are a controlling prick and Carol hates your guts. Who she chooses to see is her business. You are no longer an item, so why don't you take your threats and your boyfriend here and get back in your van while you can?

My little speech was like something Clint Eastwood might say in one of his films.

Fuck knows where that had come from.

The only other thing I could have added was the immortal line.

'Go ahead punk, make my day.'

Gary Pickering laughed and turned to Jimmy.

'Well, that sounds like fighting talk to me. What do you think, Jimmy?'

Before the other man could answer, Pickering threw a sucker punch at my head.

He telegraphed it way too much and I found myself duck under it with ease.

I dug a sharp right hook into his exposed floating ribs and followed with a left hook to his jaw knocking him on his ass.

Jimmy came forward and shaped up to me like 'Sugar' Ray Leonard.

He throw out a few half-assed jabs, which I slipped, before hitting him with a right cross on the chin that turned his legs to spaghetti.

It turns out he was more 'Sugar Puff' than 'Sugar Ray'.

Before he hit the wet grass, I landed another left hook to his jaw. He wasn't getting up any time soon.

Pickering was trying to regain his feet, but my left boot into his face prevented this and he went down again.

I now straddled his body.

Anger and hatred was flowing through my body like I had never felt.

Pickering was slipping in and out of consciousness.

I leaned my face in close to him so he could hear.

'Fucking stay away from me and stay away from Carol. If you so much as touch a hair on her head, I will find you and rip your fucking heart out. I have all the details I need from the advertising on the side of you van, so I will find you.'

With that, I dropped a headbutt onto his nose and sat back to land another right hand on his jaw.

Hopefully, when he came around, he would remember this beating for a long time.

I certainly would.

I glanced around, but nobody was about to have seen the incident.

I jogged back to the lake and washed my bloodied hands in the cold water.

They were shaking.

I had done it again. But this time, I had dismantled two guys like they were nothing.

I had to sit down on a park bench for a moment to compose myself.

Suddenly, the tears came. They were unexpected. I had no idea why.

Part of me felt once more euphoric, but another part of me felt guilt.

This wasn't Simon Winter.

The violence was too easy. It was as if it had been inbred in me all my life, but I knew this wasn't true.

I was shocked at the level of hatred and raw bloodlust in my actions.

I sat there until the tears stopped and as I began to make my way home, it was the first time I began to question who had been the man whose heart I now had in my body?

CHAPTER NINE

The following weekend Simon sat in his flat on Saturday evening idly flipping through the TV channels in hope of finding something of interest.

Andrea was there with him after coming off duty from a long-haul flight to the States. At the moment, she was taking a bath.

Eve was away this weekend visiting her mother in Gloucester who wasn't well, so he knew it would be safe to have Andrea here without their paths crossing. Simon had become a devious bastard.

Andrea suddenly appeared in a white towelling bath-robe. Her hair was held up with a smaller blue towel.

Even without her make-up on, she looked stunning, thought Simon.

She now walked bare foot into the kitchen and shouted.

'Do you want anything, love?'

'I will have a cup of tea if you are making one.'

Simon heard her fill the kettle and plug it in.

She then appeared in the doorway.

'Anything good on the box?'

Simon looked up from his channel surfing.

'Well, that depends on whether you like a load of reality show bollocks or a film that has been on about 50 times already.'

Andrea laughed.

'Can't we watch *The Voice*? That's on in a moment.'

Simon rolled his eyes.

'That programme is over-hyped, overlong and overdue to be scrapped. The only good thing about it is Sir Tom Jones.'

'Well, that is not unusual,' replied Andrea and disappeared back into the kitchen.

Simon smiled to himself.

Beautiful, clever and funny. What a girl.

A moment later, she returned with two mugs of tea and handed one to Simon.

She then sat down on the sofa next to him and curled her legs up under herself.

'I saw a good programme the other night when you were at the gym. You would have liked it. I thought of you right away. It may be on catch-up, although I can't remember what it was called.'

'Wow, that interesting, eh?' Simon resumed his channel-hopping.

Andrea playfully hit him with a cushion.

'No, listen. I am serious. It was about heart transplant patients and how some of them had said that they felt they had inherited some of their donors' traits and personality. It is a medical phenomenon called cellular memory.

There was a man on there who was a vicar, and he was given the heart of a biker. Six months after his operation, he was riding a Harley Davison around. He had never been on a motorbike in his life.'

Simon had now stopped playing with the TV remote and was listening.

Andrea continued.

'A woman in America received the heart of another woman who had been shot in the face with a sawn-off shotgun and killed by her husband. This woman didn't know this, and she kept having dreams and flashbacks about being shot. Those were just a few of the stories. Like I said, you would have found it interesting.'

Simon took a sip of his tea.

'Yeah, it does sound good. I will have to look it up and watch it.'

Although he didn't show it, Simon was intrigued by what he had heard.

Later when Andrea had gone to bed, he found the programme on catch-up TV.

It was called *Weird Science* and this episode was about, as Andrea had said, a medical phenomenon referred to as cellular memory.

Cellular memory is the idea that memories and personality traits can be stored in any individual cells or in other organs, not just in the brain. The programme spoke of a study with 47 transplant recipients and found that 6% of patients felt that their personalities had changed because of their new organ. The programme went on to give various documented cases of this with people in the medical field professing they either agreed with it or trying to disprove it.

The theory could certainly explain the radical changes in Simon's personality and behaviour.

Once the programme had ended, he fired up his laptop and keyed in 'cellular memory.'

He got lots of hits on the subject.

Simon read many of the articles.

One of them asked the question of why a memory of an incident from your childhood that you may think of that was 20, 30 or more years old is still so vivid in your mind that it seems like it happened yesterday?

It asked do you ever hear something and think it sounds like your favourite song and then start singing that song? These are memories that were formed in your brain that are replayed as a result of a specific stimulus.

For a long-time scientists believed that memories were formed, processed and sent to different destinations in the brain.

Tests were conducted. Patients' brains were electrically stimulated in different areas while they were under local anaesthesia and found that the regions that were stimulated would elicit specific memories in the patient's life.

One documented case told of a patient who had her temporal lobe stimulated and she started to hum her favourite song out loud. This suggested that the memory of this song was stored in the place where it was processed or originated.

Later this theory was discounted, but continued research has found areas of the brain, such as the hippocampus, stores our memories from the coffee we had for breakfast to the holiday we enjoyed a decade ago.

Another article claimed the theory of cellular memories states that memories, as well as personality traits, are not only stored in the brain but may also be stored in organs such as the heart.

A study done in 2009 at Harvard Medical School in Boston, Massachusetts defined cellular memories as 'a sustained cellular response to a transient stimulus.'

Simon was engrossed as he found more and more documented cases.

Other evidence suggested the best way to understand cellular memories is studying cases of organ transplants. One of the more famous cases includes a woman named Claire Sylvia. In the 70s, this woman received a heart and lung transplant from an 18-year-old boy who died in a motorcycle accident.

After her surgery, Sylvia had cravings she never had before for hamburgers and other fast foods. After some time, she contacted the family of her donor and was in shock to find that the boy enjoyed the same junk foods.

Another extreme case was an 8-year-old girl who received a 10-year-old girl's heart. After her operation, she began to have nightmares of a man trying to kill her. Her dreams were so vivid that she went to a psychiatrist who actually believed they were real.

It was found that the donor was murdered and the recipient who had the nightmares described the man in such detail that the police were able to find the killer and he was convicted of murder.

There are a few different theories on how cellular memories might work but there was no strong scientific evidence on the process of cellular memories. A lot of research is being done today not only with interaction of the brain but also other body organs.

It was nearly 2.00am in the morning by the time Simon turned off the computer.

His head was swimming with all the information. He knew that sleep would not be coming soon.

The theory of cellular memory was certainly convincing, but he needed to find out more. He decided to arrange a meeting with Aadya Sharma.

CHAPTER TEN

'Cellular memory certainly is a theory many in the medical profession support, but it needs a lot more research to be validated totally.'

'Is it something you have encountered before with other transplant patients?'

Simon was sat in Aadya Sharma's office after having arranged a meeting.

The office was small and cramped.

There was just enough room for a desk and a couple of chairs.

The rest of the room was stacked with books and files.

A small window looked out onto the main cardiac outpatients' ward at Southmead Hospital in Bristol.

It was a few days after Simon had discovered all the information on the internet.

Aadya answered his question.

'Yes. I have seen certain things and patients have reported them back to me, but nothing on the level that you have described, Simon. Some people have said they felt maybe more aggressive in their nature or crave a certain food that previously they didn't like. Things like that. But the changes you have experienced are certainly extreme.'

Simon nodded in agreement.

'Don't get me wrong, Aadya. Some of these changes are welcome. My newfound confidence has been a godsend in many ways. Getting over my fear of blood is incredible. I feel liberated in many ways. I look and feel a different man.'

'I can agree with that, Simon. From when I first met you when you were waiting for the transplant to now has been an amazing transformation. You are one of the most successful patients we have ever had. It is truly admirable what you have achieved. But maybe that is just down to your willpower and determination to live, seeing you got another chance?'

'Some of that may be true, Aadya, but how do you explain my ability to suddenly fight like Tyson Fury? That side of things frightens me. I am not sure how far I would go when that switch has been flipped. You can ask anybody who knew me before the operation, and they will tell you I was practically a pacifist.'

'That, Simon, I can't explain, and I don't think I am qualified to speculate.'

Simon smiled at her.

'I understand. I know you haven't got all the answers.'

He then lent forward in his chair.

'Aadya. You have been wonderful to me, and I wouldn't have got this far without your help.'

Aadya raised her hands a little embarrassed.

'Thank you, Simon, but it is my job. I am not so special. It works both ways. For me to be successful, I need a patient who also wants to succeed and follow my advice.'

Simon shook his head.

'You underestimate yourself.'

There was a moment's awkward silence and then Simon spoke again.

'Can I ask you something? I know I shouldn't, but I need to know.'

Aadya's brow furrowed a little.

'You can ask, but I don't know whether I can answer you. Go ahead.'

Simon took a deep breath.

'The person who donated their heart to me. You told me they were shot.'

'That's right,' acknowledged Aadya.

Simon continued.

'Can you tell me the circumstances of the shooting? Who was this guy? What did he do?'

'Simon, you know I can't give out any more personal information about the donor than I have already told you.'

'I know. I know,' said Simon.

'I wouldn't ask normally, but with all that has happened to me, I am frightened of what I might do. I don't seem to have control of my feelings or actions sometimes and that worries me. Can you not see that?'

'I understand, Simon. I truly do and I empathise with you. I will give you any support I can, but I can't reveal any more information. I am sorry. The only thing I am prepared to tell you to put your mind at rest is the person wasn't a serial killer or a crime boss.'

Simon smiled.

'Well, thank God for that at least. I take it that is all you are going to tell me?'

Aadya nodded.

'And that's your final answer, is it?' asked Simon

'I am sorry, Simon, but that is my final answer.'

Simon sighed and got to his feet.

'I am sorry, Aadya. I shouldn't have put you in that position. I'll work it out. Thanks for your time.'

'Simon, I am here for you if you need me. You know that? Maybe you should consider a holiday. Get away to the sun somewhere for a while?'

Simon nodded. 'Yeah. Maybe I will.'

He got up and headed for the door.

As he got there, he turned around.

'You sure you don't want to phone a friend on that question I asked you?'

Aadya smiled and shook her head.

'No. Final answer.'

Simon bowed his head in defeat.

'I thought not.'

On the drive home, a million thoughts ran through Simon's head. This last six months had been a rollercoaster with many ups but also a few downs.

It was these downs that concerned him.

He felt that he had two personalities battling inside his body not unlike the characters in the classic book by Robert Louis Stevenson *Dr Jekyll and Mr. Hyde*.

The dark side of Simon was a dominating force that had gradually grown stronger.

His womanising was out of hand. Andrea and Eve both deserved better and as for Carol, if he hadn't got involved with her, then her husband, no matter how abhorrent he was, would not have been battered to a pulp.

Simon had run past the spot by the park gates the next morning after the incident, almost expecting to see it cordoned off with police tape and two dead bodies lying there.

That wasn't the case, but there were still discernible splashes of dried blood on the concrete by the grass verge.

When that violence rage took over, it was all-empowering.

When Simon smashed his fists into Gary Pickering, he had wanted to kill the man.

It took every bit of his reserves to pull back.

Simon now headed towards the ring road to bring him back home.

As he contemplated the facts about his violent tendencies, a car suddenly pulled out from the kerb in front of Simon without indicating.

In a blink of an eye, Simon turned into a raging animal blasting his horn and shouting and cursing the driver in front.

Luckily for Simon, he had to turn off to connect with the ring road; otherwise, he knew he would have tailgated the car up ahead until it pulled over and then God knows what would have happened.

As he began to calm down, he decided to call Andrea. Maybe it was out of guilt as he hadn't seen her for over a week. She had been away again in Barbados or was it Bali?

His phone connected to the Bluetooth in his car and Andrea answered.

'Hello, Babe. How are you doing?'

'Simon. How lovely to hear from you! Has your work quietened down, or do you still have to stay late?'

Simon had used the ploy of work overload to keep Andrea from unexpectedly coming around to the flat as he had been entertaining Eve frequently there.

'Yeah. It is a lot better. That's why I am ringing. Do you fancy going out tonight for a bite and a few drinks?'

'I would love to. That will make a lovely change.'

'Okay. Leave it with me and I will book a table somewhere nice. Get your glad rags on and I will come for you at 7.30pm. I will order a taxi. How's that sound?'

'Perfect. I will see you then.'

Simon hung up the call and smiled.

It would do them both good to have a Friday night out on the town.

He put his troubled thoughts to the back of his mind looking forward to the evening ahead.

CHAPTER ELEVEN

Simon arrived in the taxi and picked up Andrea as planned and took her to a lovely little restaurant in Clifton Village called Alfredo's, which specialised in French cuisine.

Clifton Village is a beautiful suburb of Bristol, tucked away from the hubbub of city life and located just a five-minute drive away from the centre. It is renowned for having some of the most iconic spots in Bristol, including Brunel's famous Suspension Bridge, the Observatory and Bristol Zoo.

Once they finished their meal, as it was such a lovely evening, they decided to take a stroll down into Park Street, past the museum and university and then down to the quayside.

They stopped and had a drink in a waterfront bar. They sat by the window and watched the lights from the surrounding bars and restaurants glimmer and shimmy on the water's surface.

Simon was feeling a lot better, and his mood had mellowed.

Maybe he had let everything get to him and overreacted.

He just needed to get a grip on himself and take more responsibility for his actions.

He looked at Andrea and she looked stunning.

She was something else.

She was an intelligent, funny, and sexy lady.

Any man would be envious of Simon.

So, why was he playing around and using her?

This was just not him.

He decided he needed to make some kind of amends.

'Andrea, I am thinking of a late summer break somewhere. Maybe Cyprus or Malta. Do you want to come with me?'

Andrea's face lit up.

'That would be amazing, Simon. I think we might both benefit from some sunshine. Don't you?'

Simon reached out and gently held her hand.

'I think it is just what the doctor ordered. Over the weekend, we will go online and check out a few holiday destinations.'

It was getting late, so they decided to head back for the taxi rank before it got too busy.

As they walked through the city centre, groups of young people were queuing to go into various nightclubs.

'My God. This makes me feel old. Their night is just starting, and I am ready for bed,' remarked Simon.

Andrea laughed.

'We could always join them and show them how it's done.'

Simon put an arm around her and pulled her close.

'I have a better idea. Let's get home. I think I have enough left in me to show you a few of my moves there.'

They walked on and passed a large queue waiting to go into a nightclub called *Bubbles*.

Two door personnel were manning the front entrance waiting for their cue to open up.

Simon regarded them. One was a solid looking black man, probably in his late thirties the other was a tough looking Asian girl with jet black hair. She was younger, mid-twenties.

'This looks a busy place,' commented Simon.

'I believe it is the most popular club in Bristol and also the most infamous,' replied Andrea.

Simon raised his eyebrows in interest.

'Infamous. What for?'

Andrea looked surprised.

'The shooting, of course. Did you not read about it in the papers? It was all over the news.'

Simon thought.

'Maybe. But I don't really recall.'

Andrea was animated as she told the story.

'A guy who worked on the door was murdered here. He was shot point-blank in the head by somebody in a passing car. They have never found the killer. The doorman was an ex-boxer. I can't recall his name, but it was all a massive shock. Left behind a wife-to-be with a week or so before the birth of their first child. It was all so sad.'

The words hit Simon like a truck.

He stopped and looked at Andrea.

'You said he got shot in the head? An ex-boxer?'

'Yes. But I can't recall his name. Famous apparently.'

Simon felt a strange sensation creeping into his body.

They began to walk again.

'Are you okay, Simon? You suddenly don't look so good? asked Andrea.

As Simon got level with the front of the club, he experienced a severe pain right between the eyes and a flashing blinding light. He had never felt pain like it. White dots flashed before his vision. He then saw the face once more of the man from his dreams. It was clear as day. He was grinning evilly.

Simon felt his legs give way and he collapsed to the floor.

He was still semi-conscious but felt like he was dreaming. The pain was slowly subsiding.

He heard a male voice in the crowd saying.

'You want to get him home, darling. It looks like he has had enough.'

Laughter broke out around him.

He heard Andrea saying that he didn't drink and could somebody phone for an ambulance.

Simon then heard a voice speaking to her.

'It is okay, love. I am ringing one now. It will all be alright.'

Simon looked up to see that it was the black doorman from the club.

He felt that he recognised him. But how?

Simon then felt himself slipping into unconscious and before he blacked out, he called out the name Ethan.

Simon awoke in a hospital bed back at Southmead Hospital. As he focused on the room, he saw the worried face of Andrea sat in a chair nearby.

He then saw Mr. Kumar studying a clipboard at the foot of his bed.

Mr. Kumar noticed movement and looked up.

'Well, hello, Simon. Welcome back. How are you feeling?'

Simon smiled weakly.

'Like I have a massive hangover.'

Mr. Kumar nodded.

'That's understandable, but the medication we gave you should soon make you feel better.'

Simon reached out and took Andrea's hand.

There were tears in her eyes.

'Thank God you are alright Simon. I thought it was your heart. I didn't know what had happened.'

He squeezed her hand gently.

'It's okay, babe. I am here.'

Mr. Kumar spoke.

'You regained consciousness in the ambulance and told the paramedics that you had experienced a blinding headache before passing out. Is that correct?'

Simon nodded.

'Yes. I have been having them now and again but not this intense before. Am I okay, Doctor?'

'Well, Simon you were sedated when you were brought in, and we have done a series of tests on you. The good news is that your heart is absolutely fine. There are no worries there. In fact, since the last time I saw you, you look like a different man. Remarkable.

We did a few preliminary tests on your head and again, we have found nothing to concern us, but obviously, we would like to get to the bottom of what happened, so I am going to recommend you stay in hospital a few days whilst we run further tests, such as a MRI scan, on your head, just to see what is going on in there.'

'Well, if you are looking for a brain in there you might be hard-pushed, Doc,' quipped Simon.

Mr. Kumar smiled.

'You must be feeling somewhat better as it seems your sense of humour is coming back. Seriously though, I don't think there is anything major going on, but best to be safe than sorry.'

'Okay, Doctor. Whatever you think best.'

Mr. Kumar continued.

'Okay, Simon. Get some rest now and I will see you in the morning. Good night.'

Andrea rose to her feet and shook the man's hand.

'Thank you for everything.'

Mr. Kumar nodded.

'My pleasure, Ms Golding. Please don't stay too long he needs his rest.'

When he left the room, Andrea moved to the bed and hugged Simon.

'Christ, you gave me a scare back there.'

Simon kissed her cheek.

'I gave myself a scare, but hey, you heard what the Doc said. Everything looks alright and I will be out in no time, and we will book that holiday. Okay? Now go home. It's late. How will you get back?'

'The hospital said they would ring a taxi firm they use. It is safe. I will be fine. I will come and see you tomorrow.'

They kissed and Andrea left.

Simon lay back and went over the evening's event.

Firstly, the story of the murdered doorman and then the blinding pain and the vision right outside the club where this man was killed.

Something strange was going on and Simon knew as soon as he got out of hospital, he was going to do some internet research on his murdered man.

He had a niggling suspicion in the back of his mind. The word 'cellular memory' kept creeping to the forefront of his thoughts.

Before he finally drifted off to sleep, he found that he was gently stroking the scar tissue on his chest.

CHAPTER TWELVE

As promised, two days later Simon was released from hospital. It would be a few weeks before he got the results of the MRI scan, but other than that, he was given a full bill of health.

Andrea had decided that he should spend a few days at her place just to keep an eye on him.

He agreed. This was better than her staying at his in case she bumped into Eve. He was going to have to sort that mess out sooner rather than later.

Andrea and Simon had looked at holidays online and decided on Cyprus. They booked a seven-day break in Paphos on the Southwest coast.

Simon started back to work the following day and was welcomed back by the three staff members that worked for him.

The first morning back he had got in early whilst the office was empty and accessed his computer.

He typed in the search engine *Shootings in Bristol* and almost immediately got over a dozen hits on the shooting and murder of doorman Eddie Prince.

He had worked the door of *Bubbles* nightclub in Bristol city centre and had been an ex-cruiserweight boxer, British and European champion and had challenged, though eventually unsuccessfully, for the world title.

The story went on to talk about how last year just before Christmas Eddie was working the door and came out to address a question from an unknown woman driving what seemed to have been a BMW.

As he did this, the rear window opened, and somebody shot Eddie in the head at close range. He died instantly. He had been 45 years of age. He left behind a pregnant girlfriend who was due to give birth at any moment.

Eddie had done time in the past for manslaughter and had been a bit of a handful in and out the ring, but since meeting his girlfriend, an Ester Thomas, she had helped him clean up his act.

Another hit told how Ester Thomas gave birth on January 1st to a 6lb 7oz baby boy, who she named Eddie Jnr.

Other stories told of Eddie's boxing career and others spoke about his passion for betting on the horses and how he had become a racehorse owner.

Speculation into his death suggested he owed money to some heavy people who had put a hit out on him.

The case was still open, but the police had no new leads. They suspected the hit may have been by somebody from Prince's old stomping ground in London.

The car and its occupants were never found.

Simon read on.

Eddie was originally from London, born and bred in Stepney in the East End, and had moved down to Bristol in the last few years.

Simon studied photo images of Prince. He was dark and handsome, even with the broken nose.

It said he had a string of female companions before meeting Ester.

There was a quote from a fellow doorman named Ethan Crooks who worked with Eddie at *Bubbles*.

It read.

'Eddie was a good guy and a top-class doorman. It was a pleasure to work and learn from him. He was a gentleman until it was time not to be and let's just say he could walk the walk and talk the talk.

On the night he died, I literally stepped inside the club for five minutes to use the toilet. As I came back out, I heard the shot and Eddie was on the floor.

A dark coloured BMW had sped away into the night. I didn't get the registration.

I wish I had been there to watch his back. I miss him so much.'

There was an image of Ethan Crooks below and Simon instantly recognised him as the black man on the door of *Bubbles* the other night that had rang for an ambulance.

Simon seemed to feel he knew him. As if they had met before.

Andrea had even mentioned to him as he slipped into unconsciousness on the pavement, he had muttered the name Ethan and the black doorman was surprised and asked Andrea had he met them before to which she answered no.

Now, though, things were beginning to make sense.

Everything was pointing to the possibility that Eddie Prince had been his transplant donor.

But how could he find out for sure?

Aadya had made things perfectly clear that he would not find out who the donor was.

Over the coming days, Simon read online just about everything he could find on Eddie Prince, as well as watching his fights on YouTube. He became obsessed with the man whose heart he was sure beat in his chest.

Next Monday morning found Simon at his work's desk when the phone rang. He picked it up.

'Good morning. Property Plus. Simon speaking. How can I help?'

A woman's voice spoke.

'Hello. I wonder if you can give me a house valuation as I am thinking of putting my house on the market.'

Simon turned a page in his notebook and picked up his pen.

'Yes of course. If I can take a few basic details from you first and we can go from there.'

'Sure,' replied the woman.

'Okay. Let's start with your name and address.'

'My name is Ester Thomas and I live at 25 Sunnymead Road, Stoke Bishop, BS9 2GY.'

Simon knew the area. It was an affluent one and he had sold a house there a few months ago.

The name Ester Thomas resonated in his head somewhere, but he couldn't picture where from.

Simon could hear a baby crying in the background on the end of the line.

'I am just going to ask you a few questions about the property, Mrs Thomas.'

The woman interrupted him.

'Ms Thomas. I am not married.'

'My apologies,' said Simon.

The crying baby had Simon jumping to presumptions.

He then went on to get the details he needed on the property.

When he finished, he asked.

'Are you in this afternoon Ms Thomas? I will be in the area, and I could call in at, let's say, 2.00pm. Will that be convenient for you?'

'That would be perfect. I am working from home this week so I will see you then. I must go and attend to the baby.'

'Yes, of course. I will see you later.'

Simon hung up and put the phone back on receiver.

He looked at the details he had jotted down on his pad.

His eyes strayed back to the name. Ester Thomas. Where had he heard that name recently?

Simon went out for lunch at 12.30pm.

Before he left, he told a colleague, Alex Cosgrove, that he was taking a lunch break and then going on to do a house valuation. The address was in his desk diary. He expected to be back in the office by 3.00pm, but his phone would be on if there were any emergencies.

He walked up the high street from his office and decided he would call in the deli and get a roast beef sandwich and a takeaway tea.

As he strolled along, he glanced at the different shops and businesses.

He suddenly found himself stood outside *Safe Bet*, a bookies shop.

Simon had never put a bet on in his life.

He had done the lottery for a while, but eventually gave up as he won nothing, not even a couple of quid.

He now gazed into the window with a curious interest which he had never experienced before.

He felt the urge to go inside but knew he wouldn't know what to do if he did venture in the shop.

His mobile suddenly went off and he saw it was another client he was selling a house for.

It broke the spell and he answered it.

'Hello, Mrs Hopkins. How can I help...'

At exactly 1.55pm, Simon pulled his blue Ford Focus up outside number 25 Sunnymead Road.

He got out of the car, bringing his briefcase with him.

The house looked impressive from the front with a beautifully manicured front lawn.

It was detached and had a double garage next to it.

It looked strangely familiar.

From the details he had been given, he knew the house had four bedrooms, a garden room and a large, landscaped rear garden.

This house, he already estimated, would sell for around £750,000 to £800,000.

He walked up the gravel path and stepped onto the porch and rang the front doorbell.

Simon heard voices from behind the door and then it was opened by a small dark-haired and dark-skinned middle-aged woman.

'Yes. Can I help you?'

The woman spoke with an Eastern European accent.

Simon was just about to introduce himself when another voice from down the hallway interrupted.

'It's okay, Karaline. I will deal with it.'

The woman turned and headed back down the passageway.

Simon now saw a younger blonde-haired woman approach. She was carrying an infant in her arms.

As she came to the doorway, Simon estimated that she was probably in her thirties.

She wore a grey sweat suit. Her hair was tied back in a ponytail and there was little make-up on her face.

Even though this woman was dressed down, there was no denying that she was stunningly beautiful.

Simon hoped his mouth wasn't open too wide.

Her face broke into a warm smile.

'You must be Simon, the estate agent?'

Simon pulled himself together.

'Yes, I am, and you are Ms Thomas?'

The woman extended a slim hand.

'Please call me Ester. Do come in. That was Karaline, my live-in nanny, who you met a moment ago. And this little chap here in my arms is my son, Eddie Jnr.'

Simon wiped his feet on the doormat and followed Ester into the house.

'How old is he?'

'Nearly a year soon,' replied Ester.

They walked down the hallway and then turned left into a large open-plan lounge and diner.

He immediately felt like he had been here before.

Ester put the infant down into a wooden playpen that contained dozens of soft toys, plastic bricks and other sources of amusement for the little one.

'Would you like a tea or coffee before you start?'

'Well, if it's not too much trouble, I will have a tea please. White and no sugar.'

Ester headed to the kitchen.

'Feel free to look around, Simon. I will be five minutes.'

'Can I use your loo, please?' asked Simon.

'Yes of course. It's…

Before Ester had finished her sentence, Simon heard himself say.

'Up the stairs, second door on the left.'

Ester looked surprised.

'Why yes, it is. That's pretty impressive.'

Simon tried to cover himself.

'Sorry. Just a little game us estate agents like to play. We see so many houses I always try if I can guest where the bathroom might be situated.'

'Well, you know where it is. I will sort out the tea.'

Ester disappeared back into the kitchen.

Simon headed upstairs.

'What the fuck was that all about. How the hell did he know? Had he been here before?

No, he would have remembered. He hoped Ester didn't think it weird.

He used the toilet and returned downstairs.

Simon walked around the lounge, running an experienced eye over things.

It was decorated to a high spec without a doubt. The inside seemed to match the out.

Ester soon returned with the tea and Simon took it with him as he went around the house taking measurements and then photos with his phone.

Ester walked with him.

On the landing, Simon commented.

'The house is beautifully decorated. Did you do it?'

Ester smiled.

'No, I'm afraid neither me nor my late partner can take credit for it. We were not really cut out for D.I.Y.'

'May I ask you why you want to sell such a beautiful house?'

Ester took a sip of her tea.

'My partner and I brought the house with the view of getting married and bring up Eddie Jnr and hopefully a brother or sister here, but unfortunately, he died about a year ago.'

Simon instantly felt bad about asking as he could plainly see it was painful for Ester to talk about it.

'I am so sorry, and I apologise for prying.'

Ester held up a hand.

'It is fine, Simon. I am dealing with it the best I can, but because it was such big news, it is difficult to put things behind you.'

'Big news. I don't understand?' replied Simon.

Ester walked to a door.

'Here is his office or really his man cave.'

She turned the handle and pushed the door open.

She didn't enter herself, but gestured for Simon to go in.

Again, Simon had a feeling of déjà vu.

Simon entered and instantly was drawn to the photographs on the wall and the trophies in a glass cabinet, but most of all, to two shiny Lonsdale belts displayed on a table along with other memorabilia.

He knew in an instant who this was. He should do as he had been watching his fights non-stop for months. It was Eddie Prince, and this was his house.

Of course, now the name of Ester Thomas became clear and little Eddie Jnr.

Simon was suddenly overcome with dizziness, and he put his hand on the door frame to steady himself.

Ester came to his side.

'Are you okay?'

Simon looked at her concerned features. She was incredibly beautiful.

'May I just sit down at the desk here a second?'

Ester nodded.

'Yes, of course.'

Simon sat at the desk and just managed to place his empty mug on a coaster with the image of Rocky Balboa on it.

The room seemed to be closing in on him.

Everywhere he looked he saw images or objects belonging to the man he suspected had donated his heart to him.

Here he was, for God's sake, in his house, in his office. How crazy was that.

Surely it was too much of a coincidence that Ester Thomas had rung him out of the blue to value this house.

There must be a reason for all of this. It was like destiny. No wonder the house seemed familiar. Cellular memory.

'Are you feeling better?' Ester asked.

Simon nodded.

'Yes, I am. I am sorry I don't know what came over me. A bit of dehydration maybe.'

They made their way back downstairs.

Simon's mind was racing. He didn't know what to do.

Should he say something? But what?

They came back into the lounge and Ester gestured to Simon to sit down on the sofa.

She sat opposite him in an armchair.

'As I said upstairs, Simon. My partner was Eddie Prince. You probably heard the story. God knows it was in the tabloids enough. He was shot whilst working on the door of a nightclub. I was days away from delivering

Eddie Jnr. It was Christmas and we were looking forward to a great new year. But it never happened.'

Simon saw tears in Ester's eyes.

'I am sorry for your loss,' he said.

Ester wiped away the tears.

'Look at me. Christ, you have come to value my house, not hear my life story. It should be me that is apologising to you. Anyway. Enough to say, I moved here with Eddie because of my job. We were both from London.

My family want me to go back with the baby. I will stay with them until I find a suitable property there. My job has reassigned me if I want to go. They have been incredibly supportive.

So, I need to sell the house asap and make a clean break away from Bristol. Too many memories here for me. Eddie was cremated in Bristol, but his ashes went back to Stepney, his home, where they were buried. That had been his wish. I need to return to London so I can visit him.'

Simon nodded.

'Okay. I would say we should put it on the market for £799,999. I think you can get the asking price. If you are happy with that, we can fill in the necessary forms as soon as you like, and I can get the house up online. How does that sound?'

Ester smiled that lovely smile again.

'That sounds great. I am in town tomorrow. I could come to your office and sign whatever paperwork needs doing. Would 11.00am suit?'

Simon took his diary from his briefcase and flipped through to the current week.

'That would be perfect. Okay. I think I am done here.'

Ester led him back to the front door.

'I hope you are feeling better now.'

Simon walked out the door.

'Yes much. I came out of hospital just a week ago.

'Nothing serious, I hope,' asked Ester.

'Hopefully not, but six months ago, I had a heart transplant. I was in a bad way.'

He hadn't meant to say anything about the transplant, but it just had come out.

Ester looked shocked and her hand lightly clutched her neck.

'Dear God. How awful for you and there was I harping on about myself. I am glad you are alright.'

'Its fine, honestly, Ester. I guess we have both been through something very traumatic in our lives recently.

'Yes. I suppose you are right.'

Her voice was almost a whisper now and it looked like she was processing the information.

Simon sensed she was going to add something else but didn't.

She just said, 'I will see you tomorrow'.

Then she closed the door.

On the drive back to the office, Simon's mind was reeling. He was now almost sure Eddie Prince was the donor of his heart. Too many things were falling into place.

Before today, he had a strong belief about Prince being his donor, but after the visit to the house, he was now sure.

The truth, then it seemed, was that part of the time he was living as Simon Winter, albeit a better version than the previous one, but also, he was living the other part of his life as Eddie Prince.

If this was the case, then what did the nightmares and visions that he was having mean and how were they connected to Prince?

It was a part of the man's life he didn't know about, and it scared him.

But in spite of his reservations, one thing he was sure about was that he was determined to get to the bottom of the mystery for his own sanity.

CHAPTER THIRTEEN

At exactly 11.30am the next day Ester Thomas walked into *Property Plus* and Simon came out of his office to meet her.

Today she looked more stunning than ever.

Her blonde hair was worn loose hanging to her shoulders.

She wore a short brown suede jacket over a white blouse, blue jeans and a pair of ankle boots.

They shook hands.

'Hello, Ester, please come through to my office. This won't take long.'

Simon ushered her in and offered her a chair opposite his desk.

For some reason, he felt nervous and on one occasion even dropped his pen on the floor as he guided Ester through the paperwork to be signed.

At one point, he came around the desk close to Ester to point out a clause she had to read.

She read it and handed him back the paper.

'I know this sounds strange, Simon, but is the aftershave you are wearing by any chance *Sauvage* by Dior.

'Why yes, it is. How did you know?'

Ester looked wistfully towards the window as if remembering something.

'It was Eddie's favourite. What a coincidence.'

This was another sign for the Simon Winter and the Eddie Prince connection.

He couldn't contain himself any longer.

'Maybe it is not such a coincidence after all. Just like me knowing where your bathroom was yesterday.'

Ester looked confused.

'I don't understand what you mean.'

Simon looked at his watch.

'Ester, have you got time to nip out with me for a coffee. There is something I would like to speak with you about, but away from the office.'

'Well, I have a dental appointment at one o'clock, but yes, I can spare half an hour or so.'

'Great,' said Simon as he stood up and grabbed his jacket off the back of his chair.

Fifteen minutes later, they were sat at a corner table in Starbucks.

Ester had a flat white coffee in front of her. Simon had a mug of tea.

'Okay, Simon, what is it you want to ask me? I must admit, I feel a little nervous.

Simon leant forward in his seat.

'I am sorry, Ester. I don't mean to alarm you. May I ask you something about your husband?'

'Okay. What is it you want to know?'

'Sorry to dredge up sad memories, but when your husband Eddie died, was his heart donated to medical science for transplant use?'

'Why yes it was. Both his parents had died of heart attacks and Eddie did a lot of charity work for the British Heart Foundation. He felt strongly about the cause. Strong enough to donate his heart. How did you know?'

Simon took a deep breath.

'Ester, I think that my heart donor patient was Eddie.'

Ester was silent and looked down into her coffee cup.

Finally, she broke the silence.

'This is a lot to take in, Simon. What really are the chances of us meeting through a house sale and what you say is true?'

'I know it sounds crazy, but please hear me out first.'

Simon went on to explain about feeling he had been in her house before. About his sudden ability to box. Losing his fear of violence and blood. His sudden obsession with fitness and diet way beyond a normal person's interests.

He told her about the headaches and what happened outside the nightclub. He even told her about his nightmares and visions. Finally, he spoke about cellular memory.

When he finished, Ester pushed her half full coffee cup away from her.

'Simon, are you honestly saying that you have somehow developed Eddie's traits and personality and that you believe it is down to the fact you think that you have his heart beating in your chest?'

'That's about it, Ester. Yes.'

'That's mad. I have never heard of this cellular memory thing. A heart can't have memories, for God's sake.'

'Ester, I know this is a lot to take in. At first, I was sceptical. Look it up online. There is loads of information on it. I was told before the transplant that the man whose heart I was having was from the same part of the country as me. Also, that he had been extremely fit and healthy. I was also told that they had died from being shot. I read up on Eddie online and it all adds up.'

Ester got up from the table.

'I really don't know what to say or what you want from me.'

'Wait, Ester. I didn't mean to upset you, but I have been going mad for months and I needed to tell somebody who might understand.'

'I have to go, Simon. I will be late for my appointment. Sorry, I don't wish to speak about this anymore.'

'What about my aftershave, Ester. You told me Eddie wore the same fragrance.'

'I am sure many men wear the same fragrance. That proves nothing.'

'I only started wearing that aftershave after my operation not before,' replied Simon.

Ester was silent for a second and then she slung her bag over her shoulder.

'I have to go,' she said.

Simon tried to object, but Ester was gone out of the door and up the high street.

Simon sat with his cold mug of tea and stared out of the window. It was beginning to rain.

He wondered what damage he may have done to Ester by revealing his thoughts. Maybe he should have just kept them to his self.

But what were the chances of Eddie Prince's woman randomly out of the blue contacting *Property Plus* and he going to her house to value it.

There was a reason to all this. He was sure.

Simon also thought that it was somehow connected to the man in his nightmares.

It was as if Eddie Prince was trying to tell Simon something.

Whoever this man was Simon began to think he held the key to the whole mystery.

Simon trudged his way back towards the office. The rain was getting harder. As he passed *Safe Bet* again, he found himself drawn inside.

He tried to convince himself it was to shelter out of the rain for a while, but deep down, he knew better.

What frightened him more though is that he went straight to one the televisions that hung on the wall and looked at the betting for the next horserace, which was the 1.45pm from Kempton Park.

Then like a veteran of these matters he filled in a betting slip for the race and picked a 30-1 outsider called Punch Drunk. He had been drawn to the name more than anything.

He placed a £20.00 bet to win and watched the race. Punch Drunk didn't place in the top five.

Simon had no better luck with his next two bets and was thinking of another go when his mobile went off. It was Alex Cosgrove wanting to know if he was coming back to the office.

Simon looked at his watch and realised it was 3.00pm. Shit, he had been in the shop well over an hour or more.

He told Alex he had been held up but would be back in ten minutes.

Simon exited the shop into the daylight. The rain had stopped.

He realised that he was sweating.

What the fuck had happened in there?

Not the fact he was £60.00 lighter in his pocket than when he went in, but more to the point, where the fuck had he learnt to put a bet on?

The whole incident seemed surreal as if he had been watching himself in another outer body experience.

Now as he neared his office, he honestly couldn't remember a thing that had happened in the betting shop.

Two days later, Simon and Andrea found themselves at Bristol Airport ready to board their plane to Cyprus.

Before finishing work the previous night, he had texted Ester to say that he would be out of the country for seven days and if she needed to get in contact in relation to the house sale, Alex Cosgrove was up to speed with things.

He had received a short return text just saying *Thank you*.

Simon had wanted to say more, but he didn't know exactly how to approach the subject again. He finally decided to let the dust settle and see what would happen when he returned from holiday.

He vowed he would try to put the episode behind him for now and give Andrea the holiday he had promised her.

That shouldn't be too hard. Should it?

CHAPTER FOURTEEN

Their 4-hour 40-minute flight to Paphos International Airport landing on schedule.

Simon had been here many years back with Jean before they had the kids.

The holiday didn't go well as he caught a touch of food poisoning and spent most of the time in bed much to Jean's annoyance.

Another epic fail in his life that he wanted to forget when he was the Simon of 'old'.

Simon and Andrea took a taxi to their all-inclusive seafront hotel.

Two hours later, they were dining in the huge buffet restaurant with a backdrop through the surrounding panoramic glass windows of a setting sun over the lush green gardens and the Mediterranean beyond.

It was truly idyllic, and Simon felt relaxed for the first time in weeks.

The holiday went well.

Andrea told him that it was nice to step off a plane for a holiday rather than have to get it ready for a return flight.

Most days they strolled along the seafront and browsed the local shops in the mornings and in the afternoon, they lazed on sun loungers, read, or swam in the large warm infinity pool.

On a couple of days, they took a guided coach tour.

One to the Tombs of the Kings, a large necropolis lying about two kilometres north of Paphos harbour. It is a UNESCO World Heritage Site. The underground tombs, many of which date back to the 4th century BC, are carved out of solid rock.

The other to Coral Bay, a popular tourist resort in the Peyia municipality 11 kilometres north of Paphos. The coast to the north and to the south of Coral Bay is characterised by rocky headlands and sea caves. Coral Bay itself is a 600m crescent of soft white sand and clear blue sea.

At night, they dined on fresh fish, meats and salads and drank delicious wine, which Simon allowed himself.

They made love in the moonlight with the doors of their balcony open, allowing the scent of lemon and lime trees in the hotel gardens to enter their room.

Simon rose every morning at 6.00am and donned his running gear and went for a three-mile run along the seafront.

When he ran, his thoughts did drift to Ester. He hoped they would talk when he returned home.

He wanted her to be happy. He hadn't meant her any distress or harm.

He somehow felt protective towards her.

The headaches and bad dreams at the moment were held at bay, so was the dark side of Eddie Prince, or so Simon thought until their last day in Cyprus.

It was late morning and both Simon and Andrea were sunbathing on their loungers. Simon was reading a book. *Hands of Stone: The life of Roberto Duran.* His burgeoning appetite for all things boxing was still avid.

They had an early evening flight back to Bristol so they thought they would stay close to home and enjoy the last few hours relaxing.

Suddenly, a shadow fell across the loungers and Simon glanced up to see two men stood there.

He appraised them quickly. They looked in their late 20s. Both were suntanned and fit looking. One was blonde. The other had a smooth-shaven head. They reminded him of archetypal surfers.

He had seen them both before around the pool indulging in horseplay and trying to come onto the ladies.

Simon had already noted them down as a pair of arrogant arseholes.

When the blonde man spoke, Simon detected what he thought was a German accent.

'You seem to be lying on our loungers, my friend.'

Simon sat up and closed his book.

'There must be some mistake. These loungers were free when we found them.'

Blondie grinned and looked at his friend.

'Karl, we put our towels here before going to breakfast. Yes?'

The bald man nodded.

'Yes, we did, Jurgen. Definitely.'

Simon felt a tingle of adrenaline in his belly. He knew this wasn't going to end well, but there was no way he was going to be bullied. Not anymore.

'Sorry, guys. Like I said, you have the wrong loungers. Definitely no towels and I believe the poolside ruling is you can't reserve loungers with towels anyway.'

Both men shifted their weight from foot to foot. They puffed out their chests in a threat display just like a bird would puff out their feathers when under threat to make themselves look bigger.

The blonde guy named Jurgen moved closer to Simon.

'I suggest you and your lady here get off the loungers and go elsewhere. You really don't want to fuck with us.

By now, Andrea had sat up and said, 'It's not worth it, Simon. Let's go to the beach instead. It's no big deal.'

Simon stared at both men who, in turn, stared back.

Jurgen's features broke into a sickly grin.

'That is sound advice here from your lovely lady, Simon. I suggest you take it.'

Inside, Simon tried to keep a rein on the rising adrenaline in his body.

Somewhere in the world, he thought, is a factory churning out a long of conveyor belt arseholes. One after another.

All his life, he had hidden and cowered from the bullies. His schooldays were plagued with them.

His fear of blood and reluctance to fight had made life miserable for the young Simon Winters. But not now. This was a different Simon Winters.

He stared at both men for a moment longer and then got off the lounger.

'Yeah, you are right, love. Let's go to the beach.'

Andrea breathed a sigh of relief whilst the two men high fived each other in victory.

Jurgen turned back to Simon.

'You have made the right decis…

Before he could finish his sentence, Simon exploded a peach of a right hook onto his big square jaw.

The German's legs gave way as he sunk to the concrete.

Another right hook put him spark out on his back.

Simon then dropped low and threw a vicious uppercut into Karl's balls and followed it with a wicked hook into his kidneys. The man went to his knees in pain and surprise.

Simon now grabbed the back of his neck and repeatedly smashed his face into the edge of the lounger shouting.

'You want the lounger. Well. fucking have it then. Here you go, you fucking prick. Say thank you then.'

Andrea pulled Simon away as a crowd was beginning to gather.

'Stop. Simon, please. You will get arrested.'

She looked into his wild eyes. They were glazed over and for a moment she didn't recognise him. Then, gradually, he began to calm down.

He was sweating in the midday heat and his chest was rising and falling rapidly.

His eyes cleared and he was back.

They gathered their belongings and left the pool side before word filtered back to the management there had been trouble outside.

Back in their room, Simon went to the bathroom and stripped off his shirt and swimming trunks and turned on the shower.

He regarded himself in the bathroom mirror. He looked hard to see if he was still Simon Winter or had he morphed total into Eddie Prince.

The violence was getting worse each time. There seemed to be an anger raging inside him that he had no idea where it was coming from, but he did know it was from Eddie Prince through him.

What was it that Eddie wanted from him?

Suddenly, he was aware of Andrea beside him.

'You are one mad fucker, Simon Winter, but I do love you.'

She stripped off her bikini and guided Simon into the shower with her and pulled the curtains.

They made frantic love as the warm water cascaded over them.

Later, Simon and Andrea checked out of the hotel without incident and a couple of hours later were flying out of Cyprus and heading home.

The man was staring at Simon. The man that he had come to know in his dreams. He was middle-aged with gelled-back black hair and a face of stubble. He had a tattoo of a spider on his neck.

His hands were adorned with chunky gold rings and the faded tattoos of Love and Hate were just about visible across his knuckles.

He wore a smart black designer suit with a white open neck shirt underneath.

The man alluded threat and danger as he walked towards Simon.

As he got closer, he reached inside his jacket and produced a gun. It was black and menacing looking. Heavy calibre.

He aimed it at Simon who tried to run, but his feet seemed like they were set in cement. He could do nothing but scream as the man pulled the trigger.

Simon woke with a start and looked into the concerned features of Andrea.

'It's okay, Simon. You were dreaming. Buckle up your seatbelt. The plane is beginning its descent down into Bristol.'

Simon nodded and clipped in his belt. As he did this, he noticed that his hands were trembling.

The dreams were back and so too he noticed a gnawing headache.

CHAPTER FIFTEEN

The following week back at work, Alex Cosgrove informed Simon that they had quite a lot of interest in the property of Ester Thomas, 25 Sunnymead Road. There had been a couple of serious bids put in at the end of last week and Ester was thinking them over.

Simon thanked him and decided to give her a call and see if she had come to any decision on the sale. He also wanted to know if she had thought any more about what he had said to her prior to him going on holiday.

Simon was surprised when Ester answered and suggested he come over to the house.

So, at 11.00am, Simon, once again, pulled up outside Ester's house.

He had to admit he felt a little nervous.

Walking up the pathway, he wondered what sort of reception he would receive.

He rang the bell, and it was Ester herself this time who opened the door.

As before, her beauty took Simon's breath away.

'Wow, I like the tan,' said Ester. 'Come on in.'

Simon stepped over the threshold.

So far, so good.

On entering the lounge, Ester said.

'Karaline has taken Eddie Jnr out for a while, so we are alone. Would you like a cup of tea?'

Simon readily accepted.

He took a seat on the sofa and waited like a naughty schoolboy outside the headmaster's office.

When Ester returned with the drinks, she must have sensed his apprehension.

She handed him his tea and sat down in the armchair.

'Relax, Simon. You're quite safe. I am not going to bite your head off.'

Simon smiled.

'Well, I am glad to hear that. Only we didn't part on such good terms last time we met.'

'Yeah. Well, you kind of landed a bombshell on me, don't you think?' replied Ester.

Simon took a sip of tea.

'I guess I did. Sorry.'

Ester waved the apology away.

'Look, let's get the house details out of the way first. Your colleague Alex informed me of two good offers. One was for the asking price from a couple called the Gerrards. If they are serious, then I am happy to go with the offer.'

Simon put his tea down on the coffee table and produced his diary from his briefcase and made a note of the name.

'I will give them a ring as soon as I get back in the office.'

Ester nodded.

'Okay, Simon. Now to what you told me the other week. As I said, I was instantly shocked by what you told me, but later I did go online and read about cellular memory and the stories and experiences of people that purport to have it. They make convincing arguments,

I grant you, but medical science at this time doesn't support those claims.'

Simon went to speak, but Ester stopped him in his tracks.

'Please let me finish. You know as well as I do that, we cannot find out categorically that you have Eddie's heart. I was made aware that Eddie's heart was to be used as a donor and the hospital contacted me when that moment arrived but, like you, I knew little about its recipient. You know the strict protocol surrounding this. But let's say, for arguments sake, it is true what you say, what is it you are looking for?'

'Ester, I cannot explain how I have changed since the transplant. I know some of the changes can be put down to me being forced to alter my lifestyle, but it is other deep-seated changes that I can't explain.

I have somehow inherited the traits and personality of a man that is so far removed from who I was that it frightens me.

This man is confident, fearless, fit, and strong. A world class boxer. A hit with the ladies. Everything I am not. Yet I am.'

Simon reached in his wallet and produced a photograph of himself a couple of years ago and handed it to Ester.

'Look, that was me two years ago. I don't recognise anything about that guy in the picture. He doesn't exist no more, yet I lived as him for 40 plus years.

Christ, the other week I even walked into a betting shop for the first time in my life and betted on the horses as if I had done it for years. I haven't a clue how that happened.'

Ester looked up from the photograph.

'You bet on the horses?'

'Yes,' said Simon. 'Why? Is that significant in some way?'

Ester seemed to be struggling with her thoughts.

'Eddie gambled on the horses. The problem was he was a bad gambler and got in debt. This was before he met me. He told me all about it and he even went to Gamblers Anonymous to stop his addiction. This, he did finally.'

'Christ, Ester, another coincidence or am I onto something here?'

'I don't know, Simon. I am confused.'

Simon leant forward towards her.

'I understand how hard this must be for you, but it is also no picnic for me. I am worried where this is all going to end. The violence tendencies I have developed are getting out of hand.'

'Simon, I empathise with you. I truly do.'

'Ester, can I ask. Did Eddie have a close friend here in Bristol? Somebody maybe he could confide in if he were in trouble.'

'You think he was in trouble? If so, he would have told me.'

'Well, somebody murdered him for a reason. I don't believe he was shot randomly. Maybe he owed money to somebody? He wasn't a saint, was he, Ester?'

Tears formed in Ester's eyes.

Simon regretted the harshness of his tone. But Ester bite back.

'No, he wasn't a saint, but he was trying hard to change. I don't know why he was murdered. Neither do the police. Somebody cold-bloodedly killed the man

I loved. The father of my child and they have got away with it.'

Simon moved from the sofa to Ester and gently took her hand.

'Maybe not. Maybe this is what Eddie is trying to tell me. Surely it has got to be worth pursuing?'

Ester looked into his eyes as if searching his very soul.

At that moment, Simon wanted to hold her in his arms and tell her everything was going to be alright.

She suddenly spoke.

'Most of Eddie's friends live back in London, but down here, he was close with a fellow doorman who worked the nightclub *Bubbles* where he was shot. They were tight. Like brothers.'

'What was the man's name?'

'Ethan Crooks. He still works there.'

'Thank you, Ester. I am going to go and talk with this guy and see if it leads anywhere. I will keep you in touch of my findings.'

Ester saw him to the door.

'I can't pretend I understand what is going on here, but if you can get a lead to Eddie's killer, I will help you in any way possible.'

'Thank you,' Simon replied.

As he walked down the driveway, he saw Karaline coming up the street pushing Eddie Jnr in a buggy.

Ester called out to him as he opened the gate.

'Simon, please be careful.'

He acknowledged her with a nod of his head and walked towards his car.

CHAPTER SIXTEEN

Simon waited until Saturday to see if he could meet Ethan Crooks. He gambled on the fact that, of all the nights he would be working on the door at *Bubbles*, Saturday was going to be a good bet to find him there.

He was at his flat at present changing into a clean shirt and suit.

He found that he was spending most of his time these days at Andrea's flat. They were getting on fine and growing ever closer.

Simon trusted her and she had been incredibly supportive to him. She was a good person and he needed her in his life to keep him balanced and grounded so that it kept the dark side of him in check.

Also, the problem of Eve down the hallway had gone.

She had knocked on the door a few nights ago and was lucky to catch him as he had only popped back for some clean clothes.

She explained to him that her mother had been diagnosed with cancer and she lived alone so she was moving in with her at her house in Gloucester and would be vacating her flat by Friday.

Simon did feel sorry for her, but he was also relieved that she would be gone out of his life. That would make things a lot simpler for him as he and Andrea were now more or less a couple.

He had recently confided in Andrea his belief about having Eddie Prince's heart and how it had affected him personality wise.

He told her about the sale of Ester's house and all the strange feelings of déjà vu he experienced.

She listened without judgment.

Seeing it was Andrea that put Simon onto the cellular memory theory in the first place, she accepted that there certainly could be a high possibility of this being what he was experiencing.

He reminded her that Prince had been shot in the head and that was why he thought he had been experiencing the blinding migraines. It would also explain what happened to him outside the nightclub.

Andrea actively encouraged him to go and see this Ethan Crooks.

She also then remembered on the night Simon had collapsed outside *Bubbles* that a black man who was working the door came to her aid and rang the paramedics.

She recalled that before Simon had gone unconscious, he had muttered the name Ethan.

Surely this was the man he was looking for, but how on earth did Simon know his name without having ever met him?

When Simon learnt of this, it only added more weight to his theory.

The pieces of this jigsaw were suddenly beginning to fit together.

Simon watched from a slight distance away from the door of *Bubbles* nightclub. It was well after it had opened, and the crowd had gone inside.

He immediately spied the man he believed was Ethan Crooks. He was also the man who had helped him that night.

The black man stood with a big white guy sporting a blue mohawk down the centre of his head. They were engaged in conversation, but their eyes were watching the pavements.

Simon really wanted to speak alone to Crooks, so he waited in hope that the other man might go inside.

After twenty minutes or so, he got his chance.

He saw the white man say something to Crooks and then go inside the club.

Simon guessed he might be going to use the toilet, so he didn't have much time to spare.

He approached the club and the black man immediately spotted him and said, 'Sorry. The club's full, my man.'

Simon approached him.

'It's okay. I don't want to go in. I came by to thank you.'

The black man looked puzzled.

'Thank me. What for, bro?'

'I was the guy who collapsed outside here going back a few weeks. You phoned the paramedics.'

The man's face suddenly dawned with recognition.

'Yeah. I remember. Are you okay now? You looked pretty bad, my man, at the time.'

'Yes. I am fine now. Thanks.'

The black man smiled.

'Well, that's good news and thanks for dropping by. That was mighty Christian of you.'

Simon nodded.

'Can I ask, are you Ethan Crooks?'

The smile faded a little on the black man's face.

'Yes. I am. Why do you ask?'

'I did want to come by and thank you Ethan, but also, I would like to speak with you about Eddie Prince.'

'What about Eddie Prince?'

'Ester Thomas told me to come and speak with you.'

Ethan's eyebrows raised in surprise.

'Ester told you. What is this all about, man?'

The door opened behind Ethan and the white man with the mohawk reappeared and immediately gave Simon the eye.

'Look, Ethan, I can see you are busy right now. Can we meet tomorrow? It is really important.'

Ethan Crooks looked at Simon as if he were chewing over the request.

'What's your name?'

'Simon Winter.'

'Alright, Simon. Here is the deal. Tomorrow morning 11.30am you can meet me at *Joe's Fight Gym* in Bedminster. You know it?'

'I will find it.'

'Okay. You come to the reception and ask for me. I train there every Sunday around that time.

'Thank you,' replied Simon and he walked away.

The next morning bang on 11.30am Simon walked into the reception area of *Joe's Fight Gym*.

The gym was home to boxing, kickboxing, and mixed martial arts.

Reading up about it online, it had been established since the 80s. Local retired boxer Joe Braddock first owned it. Joe passed away some years ago and other owners had come and gone, but they all kept the iconic name in respect to the original owner.

Simon had never been in a place like this in his life, yet he felt no trepidation at all.

The old Simon Winter would have run a mile from here. The place would have just about all his fears under one roof.

Tough, violent men and woman who liked to fight, who were not afraid to give and receive punishment and were used to seeing blood. Fuck, it would have been the stuff of nightmares. You might as well have dropped him in Camp Crystal Lake with the crazed serial killer Jason Vorhees from the *Friday 13th* films.

Behind the counter was a short squat guy who appeared to have no neck. He sported two cauliflower ears and a pair of biceps that would not have looked out of place on Conan the Barbarian.

He looked Simon up and down the way a hungry lion would eye a gazelle on the plains of the Serengeti .

'What can I do for you, pal?' he said. His accent was broad Glaswegian.

Simon thought he sounded like the comedian Billy Connelly, but that was where any other comparisons ended.

'I have come to meet with Ethan Crooks. He asked me to be here for 11.30am,' answered Simon.

The man eyed Simon warily.

'What's your name, pal?'

Simon told him and the man disappeared into the gym.

This guy didn't get the job of working on the gym reception for his sparkling personality and customer care, that was for sure, mused Simon.

As he waited, Simon looked at the walls adorned with fight posters from all eras. Some now were yellow and faded. There were some famous faces there from many different combat sports.

Hagler, Hearns, Leonard, Duran of boxing, Liddell, St. Pierre and McGregor of MMA.

Simon would not have had a clue who they were six months ago.

He even spied one of Eddie Prince from way back fighting somebody called Paul 'Pitbull' Hardy top of the bill at the famous York Hall in London.

The man came back.

'Go on into the gym. Ethan is just finishing up in the corner ring.'

'Thanks,' replied Simon.

He walked into the main gym and was hit immediately with the smell of sweat, liniment and old leather.

There were two rings and a cage, all occupied with people sparring.

Rows of various punchbags were being neutralised and a wall of mirrors saw others there shadow sparring or skipping.

Simon felt an immediate tingle of excitement in his belly. He had the overwhelming urge to go to a heavy bag and punch the hell out of it.

He spied Ethan in the far ring and moved closer.

The man was certainly ripped. Sweat was glistening on his muscles as he punched, kicked and kneed a set of Thai pads that his partner was holding for him.

Simon marvelled at the speed and power that Ethan was unleashing his strikes.

Suddenly, a timer sounded, which brought the round to an end.

Ethan stopped and brought his hands up in a pray-like pose and bowed to the man holding the pads.

He made his way back to the corner and that's when he saw Simon.

'You found it then?' he asked.

Simon nodded.

'Yes, no problem. Great place. You were mighty impressive there.'

Ethan climbed out of the ring and grabbed a towel and wiped the sweat from his face.

'Not too bad,' he said.

'Well, you look like you know what you are doing,' replied Simon.

'I held a version of the British middleweight Muay Thai boxing championship belt at one time. I had over 30 fights, but the shelf life of a Thai boxer is a pretty short one and I retired at 32. I still like to train myself and also coach a few of the younger guys that come in here.'

Ethan then sized Simon up.

'Did you ever fight?'

Simon laughed.

'Who? Me? You got to be kidding. I couldn't fight sleep.'

Ethan laughed.

'You look in good shape for an old boy.'

As he said this, he flicked a playful jab out at Simon's head.

Simon instinctively slipped it with ease.

Ethan was impressed.

'Whoa, brother! I think you are bullshitting me with reflexes like that.'

Simon tried to play things down.

'Beginner's luck and too much time in my younger days playing on *Street Fighter.*'

Ethan started to pull off his gloves.

'Look, I am running a little late, so I will grab a quick shower and meet you in reception in 15 minutes.

There is a little coffee place around the corner, and we can talk there.'

'Fine,' replied Simon.

Thirty minutes later, both men sat at a window table in the small independent coffee shop called *Quick Brews.*

Both had ordered their drinks.

'So, Simon, what is it you want to know about Eddie Prince?'

Simon leaned back in his chair.

'First, Ethan, to make any kind of sense out of this, I want to explain to you what has happened to me the last year or so.'

A young girl suddenly appeared with their drinks.

She placed an Americano coffee in front of Ethan and a tea for Simon.

Both men acknowledged her with a thank you.

Ethan stirred his coffee and then said.

'Okay. I am all ears.'

Sometime later, Ethan sat back in his seat.

'Fuck, man, that is the weirdest shit I have ever heard. That is totally fucked up.'

'Tell me about it. But that is my present life in a nutshell, and it is driving me mad. I need answers,' replied Simon.

Ethan was shaking his head.

'Shit, man. I don't know what I can tell you. This is like some Twilight zone Voodoo crap.'

'Look, Ethan. I don't expect you to psychoanalyse me. What I need to know from you is why do you think somebody shot Eddie?'

'Like I told the police when it happened, I didn't see who did it and I don't have a solid reason why.

On the doors you get plenty of threats of comebacks, but hardly ever do any materialise. Once the punter is sober, they are not so brave. There can be the odd looney tune who comes looking for revenge, but fairly rarely in this country do they come armed with a shooter.

It could have been a disgruntled punter, but my gut says no. To me, it has all the hallmarks of a proper hit. Eddie had a bit of a chequered past from some of the stuff he told me.'

Simon took in this information.

'If this is the case, Eddie must have pissed somebody off big time. Somebody who was extremely dangerous.'

Ethan nodded in agreement.

Simon had another thought.

'Did Eddie ever mention he gambled to you?'

Ethan looked up from staring in his empty coffee cup.

'Funny you should mention that. Going back a while one night when we were working the doors, I mentioned to Eddie that after our shift I was going to call in at *Diamonds Casino* nearby as I was getting some luck on the poker tables.

He suddenly became serious and told me gambling was a mug's game and I should leave it alone. I told him to keep his hair on and that it was only a bit of fun.

He then replied that's what he thought at the beginning, but he got himself in some serious debt when he lived in London. He went on to say everything was okay now, but he had to even go to Gamblers Anonymous to get over his addiction.'

Simon took a sip of his tea.

'Tell me, did you take this advice?' he asked Ethan.

Ethan smiled.

'Sort of. I no longer play poker. I have moved on to Blackjack.'

Simon smiled and offered his hand.

'Thanks for talking to me, Ethan. It has helped.'

Both men shook hands.

'I am sorry I can't tell you more. What are you going to do now?'

'I am going back to have another chat with Ester.'

Ethan face became serious.

'Okay, man. Be safe. You may be unravelling a shitload of trouble for yourself. You know where I am if I can help and give my love to Ester.'

Simon nodded.

Ethan made for the door and then turned around. His face had a smile on it again.

'If you really have Eddie's heart and he is part of you, what tattoo did I get removed last year that I was always harping on about?'

Simon laughed, but in that instance, an image flashed into his head.

'I don't know. Let me guess. A rose with an ex-girlfriend's name under it. *Emma or Gemma* maybe?'

Ethan laughed.

'See you around, my man.'

Once outside, Ethan walked past the window and saw Simon now on his mobile.

They acknowledged each other with a salute.

Ethan headed back to his car deep in thought.

This is spooky shit. That motherfucker was spot on about his removed tattoo and ex, Gemma.

CHAPTER SEVENTEEN

After Ethan left, Simon phoned Ester and asked if he could come around and see her. Ester agreed but told him she would meet him in the park down the road from her house as Karaline was in today. It would be more private to talk outside.

Simon met Ester at the park gates. She had Eddie Jnr with her asleep in his buggy.

The day was fine, so they walked to the lake in the centre of the park where there was a small café.

They both sat at one of the wooden tables outside and Ester had a latte whilst Simon had another tea.

'So, how did it go with Ethan?' asked Ester.

'Fine,' replied Simon. 'He sends his love by the way.'

Ester smiled. 'That's nice.'

'Yeah. He is an okay guy,' said Simon.

'Did he help you in any way?' asked Ester.

Simon leant in close across the table.

'He told me about Eddie's gambling problems.'

Ester became defensive.

'What about them? He gave that all up when we moved here.'

Simon held up a pacifying hand.

'I know. I know. But when he was in London, apart from yourself, would there have been anybody else he would have confided in about his addiction? A friend or work colleague perhaps?'

Ester took a sip of her coffee.

'The only person I can think of would be the manager of a nightclub he worked at when we met. His name was Billy Charles. He was good to Eddie. They became close. Much more than just employer and employee.

Billy, I believe, is not well. He couldn't make Eddie's funeral last year. His wife Tanya and he sent a wreath offering their condolences. When we moved to Bristol, we lost touch.'

Simon nodded.

'What was the name of the club?'

Ester smiled sadly.

'It was called *Jester's*. How could I forget? I think I fell in love the first time I saw Eddie. I saw him on the door and undoubtedly, he looked a fighter, but he also had a gentle childlike demeanour about him.

That is what I fell in love with. I wasn't interested in Eddie Prince the boxer. Not many people got to see the other side of him, but I was one of the lucky ones.'

Tears came to Ester's eyes as she reminisced.

Simon made sure he tread carefully in this emotional moment.

He gently took her hand.

'I am sorry to have to rake up painful memories once more, but to get to the bottom of what happened to Eddie, I need to know as much as I can.'

Ester wiped her eyes with a tissue.

'I understand,' she said quietly.

'Whereabouts is the club situated?'

'It is in Soho. Off Wardour Street in Chinatown.'

'Do you have a contact number for Billy Charles?'

Ester thought for a moment.

'I don't myself. Eddie had all his contact numbers on his phone, but that is long gone. But there may be something written down or a business card in Eddie's office at home. Finish your drink and we will go take a look.'

Once at home, Karaline took Eddie Jnr, who had woken up, into the kitchen for his lunch.

Simon then followed Ester upstairs to the office.

At the door, he felt his breathing become laboured and a cold sweat beaded his forehead.

His heart rate rose, which momentarily frightened him.

He took a few deep breaths and composed himself.

Ester entered the room and he followed gingerly.

Once again, the feelings of familiarity flooded over him.

He watched almost trancelike as Ester rummaged through drawers and scoured the desk.

After ten minutes or so, she was ready to give up when Simon suddenly said.

'The boxing cup there on the shelf. The big gold one with the red ribbons. Look inside of it.'

Ester walked towards it and reached inside and there was a handful of business cards.

'Check them,' said Simon. His voice was almost a whisper.

Ester glanced through half a dozen before she stopped, and her eyes lit up.

'Here it is. Billy's business card with the address of the club and a couple of phone numbers on it.'

She then looked at Simon.

'How did you know it was in the cup?'

Simon stared blankly at her.

I have no idea. The only explanation is that Eddie led me to it.'

'Jesus, Simon. You are scaring me. Let's go back downstairs,' said Ester.

This time Simon led the way back down to the lounge.

'Now what?' asked Ester.

'I need you to ring Billy and ask if he will talk to me. I am more than willing to go up to London to meet him.'

'Okay, Simon. But I will have to do it later when the baby is in bed and Karaline isn't about.

It is a long time since I have spoken to Billy. I don't know what his health is like now. The last time I spoke to him was before leaving London for Bristol. I hope this mobile number on the card is still his.

I know he isn't just going to talk to a stranger, so I suggest we spin the story that you are a family friend who is going to write a biography about Eddie. That will take away any suspicion and hopefully get Billy to open up.'

'That's fine, Ester. I can go along with that. If you get hold of him and he agrees, then ring me straight away.'

Simon headed to the front door.

In the hallway, he stopped and turned to Ester.

'Thank you for being so understanding, Ester. I know how bizarre this all must seem. But I really think we are on to something and hopefully we can both finally get some closure.'

Ester nodded.

'I hope so too, Simon.'

Later that evening, Simon received a call from Ester telling him that the mobile number for Billy Charles had been correct.

She had spoken to his wife Tanya.

She had been pleased to hear from her. It had been so long. They had heard about the shooting and death of Eddie, but at the time, Billy had been in hospital recovering from a sudden stroke so they couldn't attend the funeral. She hoped that Ester had received the wreath that they sent, which she confirmed she had.

Tanya then went on to say that Billy and she had meant to call her or visit the memorial site, but as often was the case, time just seemed to slip by so quickly.

They no longer owned *Jester's* nightclub.

Billy's stroke had left him with speech and mobility problems.

They had sold off the club. Tanya had been a hairdresser by trade before they had got into the hospitality business, so she went back to that and opened her own salon.

Billy was all but retired these days.

They lived near Covent Garden in a ground-floor flat attached to her business.

Billy was pretty much confined to home as he could no longer drive.

Ester had explained that Simon was a friend of the family who was writing a biography about Eddie and would like to speak to Billy about Eddie's time working on the doors at *Jester's*.

Tanya told her that would be fine, and she was sure Billy would welcome the company.

But Simon would have to come to London as Billy didn't communicate so well on the phone.

Tanya gave Ester her mobile number and told her to get Simon to ring it and speak to her when he planned to come up to see Billy.

Simon thanked Ester for her help, and he told her that he would keep her up to speed with what he found out.

CHAPTER EIGHTEEN

The next day, Simon rang Tanya and made the arrangements to come up to London on the weekend.

Andrea said she would like to come with him. Simon, who was now secretly gambling, was feeling a little flush as he had just had a bit of luck on the horses and had won £250.00, so they booked a hotel in Covent Garden from Friday evening to Sunday. They would make a weekend break out of it and take in some of the sites at the same time.

They drove up to London on Friday afternoon and booked into their hotel without any problems and then dined in Covent Garden that evening and drank champagne.

They finally walked back hand in hand to their hotel.

Simon felt relaxed and happy, but in the back of his mind, he was thinking about tomorrow's meeting with Billy and what the outcome would be.

He was now getting the headaches and the flashbacks of the mystery man on a regular basis once more, and he now knew until he found out who was responsible for Eddie's death and why, he was not going to get any respite.

The miracle of having the new heart was something he praised the lord for every day. He had never been healthier and fitter. These were some of the benefits of having Eddie Prince's heart. It was the other darker traits of Eddie's he wasn't so happy about.

Recently, he was managing to balance these feelings, but he felt as he delved deeper into this mystery, the dominant dark side of Eddie Prince was getting stronger all the time.

He hoped and prayed that he would be able to control it.

The next morning after a late breakfast at the hotel, Andrea took a cab to Oxford Street to do some shopping whilst Simon went to meet Billy Charles.

He told her before she left that he would ring her later when he had finished, and they could meet back up at the hotel for an early dinner. He had then surprised her by saying he had booked two tickets to see the stage show *Hamilton*, which Andrea had been raving on about for so long.

Once Andrea had left, Simon began to walk to meet Billy.

The address of the salon and flat was about 15 minutes away.

The day was chilly but bright and sunny. The walk gave him time to clear his head and think about exactly what he wanted to ask Billy when they met.

Soon, he turned a corner and spied Tanya's salon, *Cut and Dried.*

He walked up to the ground-floor flat next door and rang the buzzer next to an intercom.

Looking up, he saw a security camera monitoring the doorstep.

He waited and finally a voice with a cockney twang sounded through the intercom.

'Alright, son. Can I help you?'

The person spoke slowly, and the words were dragged out.

'Yes, you must be Billy Charles? I am Simon Winter, a friend of Ester's. I arranged to meet you here this morning.'

Simon heard a buzzer sound and the front door opened.

'Come on in, lad, and shut the door behind you.'

Simon walked into a hallway and closed the door.

A man who he estimated was in his early 70s was sat in an electric wheelchair.

His left hand seemed paralysed, and his mouth drooped slightly downwards.

The man's grey hair and beard were stylishly cut and groomed.

He wore a powder blue shirt and denim jeans. On his feet were a pair of expensive looking Skechers trainers.

'Follow me, son, this way into the lounge. I got the kettle on unless you want something stronger. Unfortunately for me these days, with all the medication I am on, alcohol isn't an option.'

Simon followed the disappearing figure in the wheelchair.

'A cup of tea would be fine. Thank you.'

Simon found himself in a light and airy lounge. It was furnished minimalistically. The tasteful décor was light and dark greys. A large window looked out onto the street and above the sofa was a psychedelic-coloured print of Jimi Hendrix.

Billy rode his wheelchair into the kitchen and then reached for a walking stick leant against the dining table and, slowly but surely, got up and walked towards the kettle.

'My speech is a bit slurred from the stroke, but if I talk slowly, hopefully you will understand me. My left arm is fucked though.

Fortunately, I am not totally reliant on this thing.'

He pointed to the wheelchair as if it was an offensive object.

'I can walk but the legs get tired pretty quickly. Apart from all that I am right as rain.'

Simon smiled and walked into the kitchen.

'I can understand you Billy, no problem.

Do you mind me asking how it happened? The stroke.'

Billy flicked down the switch on the kettle to reboil it and reached for two mugs.

'Well, you can never be 100% sure, but it was the pressure of work and the stress it can bring.

The nightclub had been struggling and there had been money problems. The Soho area where my club was had a lot of competition. You needed to move with the times, and I was getting a little old in the tooth. I opened my first nightclub when Abba ruled the charts and Elton John had hair.

I was working all the hours God gave with no rest to keep it affluent and I guess it all caught up with me and bang, there we are. It could have been worse. I could have died. It was only because Tanya was at hand that she immediately phoned for an ambulance. It was a frightening time; I can tell you.'

'I can relate to that, Billy. I am a heart transplant patient. I nearly died myself some years back.'

Billy raised his eyebrows in surprise.

'Well, fuck me. I would never have guessed. You seem to have made a good recovery.'

'In general, yes. But I don't think you can ever fully get over something like that. Taking medication every day reminds you of your vulnerability.'

Billy nodded.

'That is true enough, lad.'

When the tea was made, the men retired to the lounge and Billy sat in an armchair with specially raised blocks under it, so it helped aid him stand back up comfortably when needed.

Simon moved to the sofa to face him.

'Great picture of Hendrix,' he noted.

Billy smiled.

'In my opinion, the greatest rock guitarist ever. I managed to see him at a live gig not long before he passed away. It was a magic experience. Music has been a massive part of my life. Hence the nightclub scene.'

He took a sip of his tea.

'Anyway, Ester tells me you are a family friend and collecting research to write a book about my old mate Eddie Prince. Am I right?'

'Yes. That's correct. I wonder if I could ask you about his time on the doors at your club. I believe you became good friends.'

Billy eyed Simon.

'What publisher do you work for then?'

This caught Simon a little off guard.

'I am working independently and going to self-publish.'

'Wow. That is an ambitious thing to tackle. Have you written any other books?'

Simon felt himself get a little hot under the collar.

'No, this is my first try.'

Billy took this in and nodded.

'I take it you must be a big boxing fan then?'

'Yes. I sure am.'

'Favourite all-time boxer?'

It was lucky that he had, in recent times, took an interest in boxing; otherwise, he would have been dead in the water.

'Marvellous Marvin Hagler.'

Billy smiled.

'Ah, what a great light heavyweight champion. Sadly missed.'

Simon knew Billy was testing him.

'Middleweight champion, you mean.'

'Yes, of course he was. The old mind doesn't work as well as it used to. I liked him too. Great win over Sugar Ray Leonard to finish his career.'

'Yes, indeed,' Simon agreed, but slightly worried that he might have messed up.

Billy didn't seem to flinch.

'Well then. Eddie Prince was a solid gold geezer. A pro in the ring and a pro on the door. I had been a big fan of his long before he turned up at *Jester's* looking for work.

I travelled to Las Vegas to watch him fight for the world title. James Toney was a class above that night, but if it had been any of the other crop of cruiser-weights around at that time, Eddie would have won the belt.

I couldn't believe it years later when he was stood there in front of me at the club asking for a job.'

Simon had come armed with the props of a pad and pen, and he made a pretence of scribbling down notes.

'Tell me, Billy. This man was an extraordinarily successful boxer and, for a time, television celebrity. Why did he come to do door work?'

'Well, after he came out of prison.'

Billy stopped.

'You know about the prison bit, I take it?'

Simon nodded.

'Yes. Do carry on.'

'Well, as I said, when he came out of prison, all the TV work dried up. Nobody would touch him with a barge pole. He tried to make some investments, but they all went tits up as well. He lost a lot of money. In fact, nearly all of it. So, he looked for work using the only skills he possessed. It was a big comedown for him. But as I said, he was a gem and just got on with it. For all the fame, he had he never forgot his roots.'

'Was there any truth in the rumours that Eddie had gambling problems?'

For a moment, Billy hesitated, as if considering how much he wanted to disclose, but then carried on.

'Yes, he did. The nags, you know, horses mainly. He was a gambler certainly and not a good one. He got himself into debt. I bailed him out a few times myself and he promised he would clean up his act, but he couldn't. The debts piled up and he owed a lot of money to some heavy people.'

As Billy said this, he subconsciously looked at his legs and began to rub his knees.

He seemed to be struggling with what he wanted to say.

'Look, son. The only reason I am talking to you is that Ester said that you were a trusted friend.

Now whatever you write in this so-called book, I don't want you rubbishing Eddie. Or quoting me saying anything detrimental to his memory. You understand?'

Simon nodded.

'I perfectly understand, Billy. But I would like to get to the truth as to why Eddie ended up shot dead in Bristol, even if it is just to give closure to his family.'

'I am going to tell you something. Something that nobody else except my Tanya knows. But you cannot quote me on it or speculate in your book about this.'

Simon felt his heart flutter. He felt Billy knew something important.

'Eddie owed money to a local debt collector up here. He is a nasty piece of work. A man named Archie Castle. He has his finger in many illegal pies, but money lending is his forte. He feeds on the helpless and the desperate.

His cronies or him will hang around betting shops, casinos, card games, the dog tracks, waiting and watching for the losers and then they approach them with a way out of their problems by lending them money. The interest rate is extortionate, but if you are desperate, you will grasp at anything.

If you take him up on his offer, then he has got you. If you miss a payment, you will have a visit and be warned. If you miss another something gets broken. If you still don't get the message well... you get the picture.

Castle is well known to the coppers, but word is he has a few of them in his pocket, so he has not been convicted of anything serious. He is Teflon, you know, non-stick.

When the investigation moved from Bristol to London, things suddenly stalled and then it all went cold.

Word on the street was the cops knew Castle was the shooter, but there was no proof. Plus, they didn't dig too hard.'

Simon felt excitement in his belly as the tale unfolded.

Billy continued.

'Eddie owed Archie a pretty penny and he had called the debt in more than once, but Eddie didn't have the money to pay him.

In the end, Eddie was ignoring him, and the word went around the manor that Eddie was taking Archie for a mug. Archie couldn't have that. Not in his business; otherwise, every chancer and wide boy would be trying it on. So, Archie had to send out a loud and clear message not just to Eddie, but the whole manor.

One evening, a few of his boys came to the door of *Jester's* and confronted Eddie with the final ultimatum: pay up or face the consequences. To reinforce their message, they flashed their shooters. It was all getting very heavy.

Eddie told them to fuck off. He also said to get rid of the guns and he would fight the three of them there and now, but they weren't going to get drawn into that.

Although Eddie showed some balls that night inwardly, he was worried as he couldn't see a way out of the situation in was in.

Then his guardian angel appeared in the form of Ester Thomas. Eddie was smitten. Once they were an item and living together, she was offered a job position in Bristol. Eddie saw it as a perfect opportunity to disappear out of London and the grip of Archie Castle.

Don't get me wrong, Eddie loved Ester, but the situation also solved his problem, or so he thought.

I was the only person he told where he was going. He swore me to secrecy. He gave me a phone number and address I could get in touch with him on, but only in an emergency. Then he vanished.

Archie Castle was not a happy man, and he went around all Eddie's known friends and haunts, asking questions the only way he knew how: with menace and violence.

My name was eventually put in the frame, and he came visiting one night at *Jester's*.'

The older man took a deep breath. Simon could see the memories were painful.

'Take your time, Billy,' he said.

Billy glanced to the sideboard.

'Here, lad. Fuck the medication. In that sideboard is a bottle of scotch. Pour me a large one, will you?'

Simon did what Billy asked and when he handed the man the glass, he noticed that his hand was shaking badly.

Billy took a large gulp of the fiery liquid and let it settle in his stomach before continuing.

'They asked if I knew Eddie's whereabouts. Of course, I said no, but Archie wasn't taking no for an answer. He believed I was the one and only person who Eddie would tell where he was going. So, to persuade me to talk, he got one of his thugs to smash my left knee with a lump hammer.

The pain was like nothing I ever felt, but I didn't talk. I am a fucking geezer; you know what I mean?

The right kneecap went next, and I was now drifting in and out of consciousness.

They were going to start on my elbows next and then the threat was they would do the same to Tanya.

I couldn't have that. She means everything to me. We were childhood sweethearts. I didn't want to sell Eddie out, but I had no choice. So, I gave up Eddie's number and address.

I was fucking helpless.

You see, the stroke partially has me in that fucking wheelchair, but those bastards gave me two artificial kneecaps as well. I couldn't walk properly before the stroke. My life was ruined.'

Simon saw tears come to the older man's eyes.

He wiped them away.

Simon looked at Billy.

'So, you suspect Archie Prince tracked Eddie down to Bristol and he shot and killed him because he ran away from the debt he owed?'

Billy emptied his glass.

'Yes, I fucking do, but I have no proof. After Eddie's death, the police came and asked me the same question. God, how I wanted to tell them that I thought it was Archie Castle, but that night, they maimed me, he told me in no uncertain terms if I mentioned anything about this to anybody, especially the Old Bill, he would come back and kill Tanya and me. So, I said nothing.'

'So, why tell me now?' asked Simon.

'Because I am 73 years of age and the doctors have told me I am unlikely to see 75. I didn't quite tell you the truth about my health earlier. You see when I was in hospital with the stroke, they did loads of blood tests on me and one of them showed that I have liver cancer. Its incurable. So, if another stroke doesn't get me first, the cancer will. I now have fuck all to lose.'

'I am so sorry, Billy. That is terrible.'

Billy regarded Simon balefully.

'Life can be a pisser, boy. That's for sure. Anyway, Tanya and I are off next month to our villa in Spain. She will get somebody to manage the salon to give herself a little income, but to all intents and purposes, I will see my time out in Malaga. Archie Castle will never be able to touch me again. So, fuck him.'

Simon nodded.

'Thank you for your time, Billy. You have been really helpful. I know that couldn't have been easy.'

Simon got up to leave.

'Hey, lad. You aren't really writing a book, are you?'

'Why do you say that?'

'Because I know that some big publishing houses have been looking for Eddie's story for the last year and Ester hasn't been interested. They have offered her a lot of money, but she has resisted it.

No disrespect, son but your name doesn't exactly ring a bell and you don't work for a publishing house, so why would Ester want you to write Eddie's life story?

Plus, anybody who knows their boxing knows Leonard beat Hagler in that fight.'

Simon smiled.

'That stroke hasn't messed with the sharpness of your brain, has it, Billy?'

Billy pointed to his feet.

'Down there for dancing.'

Then he tapped his temple.

'Up here for thinking.

So, what's your angle. Obviously, Ester trusts you, so why the cock and bull story?'

'Because we didn't think that you would speak to me otherwise.'

'So, son what is your personal interest in the death of Eddie Prince?'

Simon poured Billy and this time himself a fresh whisky.

'Because I am convinced that I have his heart beating inside of me.'

'You better sit back down and explain yourself,' said Billy.

Billy listened as Simon related his story right from the beginning. All the consequences, his personality changes, his ability to box and fight. He left no stone unturned.

Billy listened without interruption until Simon had finished.

'Fucking hell, boy. That was one hell of a story. No wonder you didn't want to come straight out with it.

But as crazy as it might sound, since my stroke I have read a lot about the effects that it can have on an individual's personality, but those facts are based on the way that a stroke affects the brain, which kind of makes sense.

I have read about cellular memory, but most medical professionals reject the theory.'

'That is true, Billy, but there are many case stories that can back up the theory,' argued Simon.

Billy smiled.

'Well, you could say that about UFOs, Big Foot and the Loch Ness Monster also, but there is no hard evidence.'

Simon got up and walked to the window and looked out at the traffic.

'I get these severe headaches that cannot be explained. The pain explodes right between my eyes and when I get it bad, I can collapse. Eddie was shot straight between the eyes, and I didn't know this to sometime after I was experiencing them.

Also, I have constant dreams of a man. A man with a gun that I have never met before, but after what you have told me, I suspect it is this Archie Castle.

It seems to me that Eddie is trying to tell me something and it is driving me insane.'

Billy shook his head.

'Son, Eddie Prince is dead. His ashes are buried in Saint Mark's churchyard in Stepney, a stone's throw from the house he grew up in. He is gone.

I can see you are upset, lad, but even if what you say is true, what do you plan to do? As you have told me, you aren't a hardman or a criminal. You wouldn't last five minutes if you went after this Archie Castle. He is fucking dangerous.'

Simon turned to face Billy.

'A while ago, I would have agreed with you. I wouldn't have gone in a million miles of this man, but now I am not so sure. Maybe this is the only way that Eddie will be at peace and also me. Where does this Castle hang out?'

Billy shook his head.

'Hey, son. You don't find Archie Castle; he finds you. He owns a club in Soho, but you don't just walk in there and ask for him.

So, my advice is leave it, son, and go back to Bristol and forget it. Whatever you're feeling will eventually pass. You don't want to go there.'

'So, you are not going to tell me then?'

'No, I am not. I don't want anything to do with it. I am totally gutted about what happened to my old friend and I would love to see Castle get his comeuppance, but you, son, aren't the man to do it. You will end up like Eddie.'

'Okay, Billy. I respect that. I will find him myself. I can't leave it.'

Billy looked sad.

'Well, remember that story about the dog that chased fire engines every time they came down its street. One day he caught up with one and didn't know what to do with it.'

Simon smiled.

'Very philosophical.'

He moved towards the older man and extended his hand.

'Thank you for your time and take care of yourself.'

Billy shook his hand.

'You too son. You too.'

As Simon released his hand, a strange feeling washed over him as he saw the watch on Billy's wrist.

He suddenly feel cold and clammy, and a vision sprung into his head.

'Are you alright, son?' asked Billy.

Simon stepped back and the feelings disappeared.

'Yes, I am fine. Billy, that watch you are wearing.'

Billy looked at the watch and then at Simon.

'Yes. What about it?'

Simon smiled as he zipped up his jacket.

'Eddie Prince bought you that for your 65th birthday, didn't he?   On the back it is engraved: *to a special friend, love Eddie.*

Billy stared open-mouthed at Simon.

'How the fuck did you know that?'

Simon walked towards the hall.

'I didn't, but Eddie did. I will see myself out.'

CHAPTER NINETEEN

When Simon left Billy Charles' flat, he had time on his hands before meeting Andrea. He walked through Leicester Square and found himself in Wardour Street. He seemed to know this area, although he had never been there in his life before.

He took a left-hand turning into Halsbury Street and there in front of him was *Jester's* nightclub.

It was almost as if he had found it on autopilot.

The building was shut and boarded up. Simon walked up to the front entrance.

The same feeling washed over him as he had felt when he saw Billy's watch.

He had been here before. It had a familiar feel. Obviously, Eddie had been here.

Simon stood on the steps outside the door of the club.

He could imagine the crowds waiting in line to come in and the throbbing boom of the music from inside.

It felt so real.

He imagined Eddie seeing Ester for the first time and how he must have felt.

He suddenly saw a couple of policemen walking along the pavement on the other side of the road and it broke the spell. He walked back down the steps and headed towards Leicester Square.

A few streets away from the club, he passed a betting shop and was drawn inside to have a punt on the horses.

Maybe his luck would change.

He had found his gambling getting increasingly more addictive.

Try as he might to stop it, he just couldn't. He loved the buzz he got from it, although he had not won big for some while.

At night, he would lie in bed and tell himself he would stop. That it was a mug's game, but the next day would find him either in the betting shop or online gambling on his phone.

He could understand now how Eddie had dug himself a hole.

Simon didn't owe money as yet, but he was getting through his savings in his bank account faster than he would like.

An hour later and 100 quid lighter, he ripped up his betting slip as he watched on the TV monitor his final horse come in fourth. He sighed and put his head in his hands. *What a fucking muppet he was.*

Suddenly, a voice nearby said.

'Never mind, son. You win some, you lose some. There is always another day.'

Simon looked up and straight into the face of the man who had been haunting his dreams.

For a moment, he thought that he was dreaming again, but then realisation hit him.

No, here was the man in the flesh.

He managed to keep a rein on his emotions.

It was, without doubt, him. The spider tattoo on his neck was a dead giveaway.

'Bad day at the races, eh?' said the man. His face broke into a grin that reminded Simon of a great white shark.

Simon steadied his voice.

'You could say that. My luck is well and truly rotten at the minute. I just need a break. But I am financially embarrassed to say the least.'

The man moved closer to Simon.

'I can relate to that. You aren't the first nor will you be the last.

Look, if you need cash, I can help. The name is Archie Castle. I am a local entrepreneur in the area. One of my specialities is that I am a money lender. I am your listening bank, so to speak. You talk I listen.

Look, you seem to need a leg up. I can provide that for a price, of course, but unlike a bank, I am always open for business.'

Simon tried to keep a rein on his emotions because he was experiencing total hate for this man.

It took every ounce of his power not to lunge and put his hands around his throat.

He had never felt such loathing towards another person.

Castle handed Simon a card.

'Look, think it over. Here is my business address and mobile number. If you need a loan, you know where to find me. Ok. No obligation. But if you have money problems, I am your fairy godmother and Santa Claus rolled into one.'

Simon took the card. He hoped Castle didn't see the tremble in his hand.

'Thank you. I will bear it in mind.'

'Not from around here, are you, son? Can't quite place the accent.'

Simon knew he had to be cautious and not mention Bristol as it might trigger suspicion with Castle.

'No. I am from Gloucester. I am up here for a long weekend with my missus.'

'Ah. I thought I detected a Southwest burr in your voice. Well, like I said, my offer is there if you want it. I don't just deal with Londoners. My reach stretches far and wide.'

'Well, thanks again,' said Simon.

He left the betting shop on unsteady legs. Suddenly, the pain in his head hit him hard and he staggered into a side alley by the shop to steady himself.

Simon's heart beat fast and he felt shortness of breath.

He began to panic.

Was he having another heart attack? Was this it?

Gripping tightly to a rubbish dumpster, he lowered his head and concentrated on trying to slow down his breathing.

He then felt nausea rising and he retched onto the floor.

Simon leant on the dumpster waiting for the feelings of sickness to pass.

Little by little, he slowly regained his breath, and his heart rate began to drop.

Five minutes passed and he felt a lot better.

Had it been a panic attack?

Simon knew whatever it had been it had been triggered by the unexpected appearance of the man from his nightmares that he now knew was Archie Castle.

He looked at his watch and realised that he had time to go back to the hotel and shower and change. He needed to do that to feel human again.

Suddenly, he became aware of the presence of somebody else standing in the alley watching him.

He looked up to see to youths. Both were dressed in hoodies and baggy tracksuit bottoms.

Simon could not make out their features.

What he did see though were the knives in their hands.

One spoke.

'Yoh, Dad, what you are doing in here? You are out of your territory, man.'

Simon knew whatever he said would not make any difference as these two scumbags were on a pre-cursor to mugging him at knifepoint.

Suddenly, everything that had gone on in the last few hours came to a head and he felt a rage consume him.

He walked towards the youths and snarled.

'Get the fuck out of my way, you pair of wankers, or I will shove those knives up your fucking asses.

If you fancy a go, then come on because I am having a bad day and you are only making it worse.

So, what do you say? If you want a piece of me, then come on, but I promise you, I will put you both in hospital without raising a sweat.'

The two youths regarded each other. This wasn't how it normally played out. Most people shit themselves when the knives came out and willingly handed over their valuables.

Not this guy though. He was off his nut.

Simon now had picked up a piece of wood from a broken pallet which lay on the ground. It had a couple of nasty looking four-inch nails protruding from it.

He faced the two youths down.

'Well, you pair of losers. Do you want it or what?'

The two would be muggers took one last look at Simon and then they both did a runner.

Simon threw the piece of wood down and stepped out of the alley.

He felt like Dirty Harry from the Clint Eastwood movies.

He laughed out loud as he started to walk back to his hotel.

Fucking hell, he had always dreamt of doing something like that. Eddie, you are a bad man.

The lines were now getting blurred to where Eddie finished, and Simon started.

When Simon got back to the hotel, he rang Andrea. She told him she was waiting for a cab and would be back soon. She asked him how it went with Billy Charles, and he said that he would fill her in later over dinner.

Once off the phone, Simon went and showered and shaved.

Dressed in a white towelling dressing gown, he felt much better.

He went to the mini bar and took out a bottle of Famous Grouse whisky and poured it into a glass.

Simon had hardly drunk alcohol since his heart transplant, but this evening he felt like it.

He sat on the bed and picked up the business card that Castle had handed him earlier on.

The card was for a club called *Lacey's*.

A little look at Google on his phone found *Lacey's* to be a Soho strip club.

It looked like Castle ran his business out of it.

No doubt it was a front for his other shadier dealings.

Simon took a sip on his drink and leaned back on the pillows.

He could not believe he had just run into the man who had haunted his mind for so long.

It was almost as if it had been meant to be.

He now felt inside a feeling of finality.

Archie Castle was the killer of Eddie Prince and Eddie wanted revenge and retribution.

Simon Winter was the vessel that it was going to come through.

Simon emptied his glass and went to the mini bar for another.

He heard the room door click and it opened, and Andrea breezed in armed with some designer shopping bags.

'Just in time, I see. I could murder a G&T, love.'

Simon put his brooding thoughts to the back of his mind. He wanted to give Andrea a special evening.

He fished out a bottle of Gordon's.

'Coming right up, Madame. I will run you a bath next. Now sit down and tell me about your day.'

Andrea kicked off her shoes and accepted the drink.

She plonked down into an easy chair.

'As long as you tell me about your day later, as promised.'

Simon smiled and made an X gesture on his chest.

'Cross my heart and hope to die.'

CHAPTER TWENTY

'You can pop your shirt back on now, Simon. Everything seems fine. Your continued progress is amazing,' said Aadya.

It was Monday morning and Simon was back in Bristol and at the hospital for one of his routine check-ups.

As Simon buttoned his shirt back up and began to fix his tie, Aadya asked him if he had experienced any more fainting fits or headaches.

He decided to play his cards close to his chest as in his mind things had changed now.

'No. Nothing. I have been great.'

Aadya sat down at her desk and gestured for Simon to take a seat.

She typed in some information on her computer.

'Good. Your MRI scan you had when you were admitted into hospital a little while ago came back to us clear.

So, in that case, you get a clean bill of health. Your meds seem to be doing what they should, so I think we are about done here.

I would like, if you can before you go, just to fill in a few forms for me. It won't take long.'

'No problem,' answered Simon.

Aadya handed him two forms.

Just then, there was a knock on the office door and a nurse entered.

'Sorry to interrupt, but I really need you to come and take a look at a patient for me. I would like a second opinion if possible. I wouldn't bother you, but I can't find a consultant on the floor at present.'

Aadya looked at Simon.

'Are you okay to fill these in? I won't be a minute.'

'That's fine. Go ahead.'

Aadya excused herself.

Once she had left, a thought crept into Simon's head.

He got up from his chair and went to the office door and opened it slightly and saw Aadya disappearing down the corridor.

He shut the door and moved back into the room and around the desk to the computer screen which had been left on.

He studied the files on the desktop screen and began clicking way.

A few moments took him to a file entitled *Heart Transplant Patients*.

He opened the file and scrolled down the names until he hit the *W*s.

There he was: Simon Winter.

He opened up his information. His eyes searched for what he was looking for and there it was the words '*Donor*'.

His hand shook as he clicked on the link.

He glanced towards the door, praying he would have time.

The link opened to reveal what he had always knew, but seeing it there now in black and white made him grip the desk tightly as his legs felt like jelly.

He stared at the name: Edward John Prince.

Simon heard voices in the corridor outside.

He quickly shut the files down returning the computer to the home screen. He then moved around to sit back on his seat and filled in the forms which had been given to him.

The door then opened and in came Aadya.

'Sorry about that. Bloody staff shortages as usual.'

Simon smiled hoping that this face didn't betray any guilt.

'Forms are all done for you.'

Aadya took them.

'Thanks, Simon. Right, sorry to keep you. If you haven't anything else to ask me, then I will be in touch again in a few months' time. So, are we all good?'

Simon got to his feet. He slipped on his jacket.

'Never better. Thanks. In fact, I feel on top of the world.'

Simon drove back home finally armed with the information he needed. He did have Eddie Prince's heart and through cellular memory, he had incredibly inherited many of his traits from personality to abilities.

People could choose to believe him or not, but he no longer cared.

He knew the truth.

Eddie Prince was living through him, and he needed help.

The visions and nightmares he had been having now made sense.

Eddie was trying to tell him the identity of his killer and that person was Archie Castle.

A revenge execution for taking his money and not paying it back.

Eddie had paid the ultimate price for his gambling debts.

Eddie Prince had certainly fallen from grace the hard way.

Simon now thought of Ester and Eddie Jnr.

They had suffered just as much in their own way.

Should he tell them about his discovery, or should he just let it lie?

Suddenly, he now had a sense of acceptance wash over him.

There was a reason he had survived his heart attack and a reason that he had been given Eddie's heart.

Before his transplant, his life had been going nowhere.

A failed marriage, a boring job, no ambition, no pride in his appearance, no confidence.

He hadn't been living; he had been surviving and kidding himself he was doing alright.

He had been a man with so many hang-ups and fears he might as well have been dead.

But after his transplant, it had been different. For the first time in over forty miserable years of his life, he felt alive, reborn.

Yes, part of him was still scared of what he had become, but another part was exhilarated.

Now he knew why this had happened.

He had a job to do. A task to fulfil.

Eddie knew the police weren't going to help.

So, Simon had become his salvation.

His ultimate challenge now lay ahead.

The reason that he was still here on the planet.

A calmness washed over him.

He switched on the car radio just in time to catch the thumping drum solo on Phil Collins, *In the Air Tonight.*

He fucking loved that song.

There definitely was something in the air and it would be coming soon.

Simon let himself into his flat. He knew it would be empty as Andrea was away for the week on flight duties.

He made himself a cup of tea and a tuna sandwich and sat down on the sofa.

As he ate, he turned over everything in his mind.

He had finally joined up all the dots to the pieces of information that had been floating around in his head for months.

His mobile buzzed and he took it from his coat pocket. He saw that it was Alex Cosgrove ringing.

Simon pressed the answer button.

'Hello, Alex.'

Alex immediately spoke.

'Just wanted to know if you were coming back into the office today, Boss, what with your hospital appointment and all that.'

Simon thought about this for a moment and then answered.

'No, I won't be back. I don't feel so good after all the poking and probing,' he lied. 'I may have to have my medication changed. I am going to take the rest of the day off and see how I feel in the morning. I will let you know.'

'Okay. No problem. Just before you go, I wanted to let you know we have now had a firm offer on the house at Sunnymead Road. Full asking price and the couple are cash buyers, ready to roll. Do you want me to tell the client?'

Simon saw this as a golden opportunity to speak to Ester.

'No, Alex. I will ring her and let her know. Thanks for informing me and well done on the sale. I am sure Ester will be over the moon. I will speak soon.'

Simon finished the call and immediately phoned Ester.

It went to answerphone, and he left a message asking if it was okay to pop over. He had some good news for her.

Simon went to the bedroom and changed into his running gear and then drove to the park.

As he began his run, he realised that he had left his mobile phone on the sofa at home.

Later when he got back to his flat, he checked his phone and found a couple of miscalls from Ester and finally a voice message telling him to come around this evening at 7.30pm.

Simon showered and dried himself in front of the full-length wardrobe mirror then wrapped the towel around his waist.

There had been a time where he would not have considered looking at himself in a mirror full stop especially if he had been naked.

Even if he had been offered a million pound and a night of passion with Rita Ora and Rhianna together, it wouldn't have happened.

Now he couldn't help marvelling these days at the shape he was in.

His daily dose of sunbed had almost eradicated any sign of his scar without really searching for it.

His chest was firm, abs tight and he had a healthy set of biceps on him.

He smiled to himself, and shadow boxed for a few moments.

Simon then walked up close to the mirror and studied his features.

If he looked really closely past the tan, designer haircut and stubble he could just make out the fat Simon, the scared Simon. Simon the loser.

But little by little, every day, that Simon was disappearing fast.

Inside of him beat the heart of a totally different beast.

The heart of a man from the other side of the tracks.

A man who had been a winner. A man who had lived life close to the wind. A man who embraced discomfort and fear. A man who wasn't afraid of anything or anybody.

Now more than ever he needed that man.

Because Simon Winter was going to kill Archie Castle so Eddie Prince could rest in peace and his death would be avenged.

CHAPTER TWENTY ONE

On the drive over to Ester's, Simon had decided not to tell her what Billy had mentioned about suspecting Archie Castle being the man who had killed Eddie.

It would not benefit her to know this. She would want to involve the police and Billy was not going to stand in court and give evidence. Also, there was no hard evidence to tie Castle to the murder. A good lawyer would have him off in no time.

Billy already bore the scars of coming up against Castle. All the man wanted now was to see his final days out in the sun. Simon respected that.

The house was sold, and Ester could return to a fresh start in London away from the final sad memories of her time in Bristol.

He had wished he had never told his suspicions to her about having Eddie's heart, but at the same time, he believed that it was fate that had brought them together and without her telling him about Billy Charles, he would not now be armed with the knowledge he had.

He didn't want to cause her anymore grief than he already had.

'So, the trip to London was a waste of time then?' asked Ester.

'Yes. Billy told me he hadn't heard a word from Eddie since he left for Bristol. Obviously, he had heard about the shooting, and he suspects it was some crazy disgruntled punter that had a score to settle with Eddie. It does happen.'

They were both sat on the sofa. Eddie Jnr was in bed.

Ester picked up her glass of white wine and took a sip.

'So, what now?'

Simon knew she would ask this. He had thought carefully how he would answer.

'I went for a check-up at the hospital the other day. Just routine. I am fine. When the nurse who checked me had left her office for a few moments, I took the opportunity to get onto her computer and found my notes. I can 100% confirm to you that Eddie was my donor.'

Ester put her glass down on the coffee table.

Simon noticed she missed placing it on the coaster.

A look of shock was on her face.

'My God, what a consequence that we met up. What are the chances of that happening? One in a million, I suspect. Jesus, its uncanny. It's like something you hear about on programmes like *Unsolved Mysteries* or something like that.'

Simon nodded.

'I know, it is unbelievable. But I now believe Eddie used me to help you. He wanted me to sell your house and make sure you and your boy are safe. He wants you to go home and be near him. I was like a kind of vessel to do his will.

I now understand this, and I accept that by selling your property I have fulfilled his wish for you. It is over.

At the end of the day, I am an estate agent, not Inspector Morse.

I don't know how long I have to live and how long Eddie's heart will give me life, but I am willing to share my life with him. I have no other choice.'

Tears formed in Ester's eyes.

Simon found himself putting a comforting arm around her.

She hugged him close as she gently wept into his shoulder.

Holding her so close and smelling her perfume threw up a whole gamut of emotions inside of him.

Part of him felt he had known this woman all his life. Another part of him knew the best thing now was for him to leave and not complicate matters further.

As Ester looked up into his eyes, every fibre of his being wanted to kiss her lips, but something was pulling him back.

'I really should go now, Ester. It has been a pleasure to meet you and I am sorry if I have dredged up too many bad memories or given you false hope. At least I have sold your house for you, and you now have an opportunity to find a new life.'

'What about you, Simon? What does the future hold in store for you?'

'I honestly don't know, Ester, but I am just grateful I wake up to another sunrise. For now, that will do me.'

Ester smiled sadly and kissed him softly on the cheek.

She showed him to the door.

'Alex will finalise everything with the house in the next week or so,' said Simon.

'Thank you, Simon. For everything. I am sure Eddie would have been happy that his donated heart went to a good man like you.'

Simon smiled.

'Maybe. Have a good life Ester and take care.'

He turned and walked down the garden path.

At the gate, he paused and looked back.

The front door was shut.

CHAPTER TWENTY TWO

The next morning Simon rang into work and told Alex Cosgrove that he wasn't feeling well and wouldn't be in for a few days.

Later, he phoned Ethan Crooks and asked if they could meet up. Crooks told him that he was training down at the gym and would be free around 1.00pm. He told Simon to get his training gear together and come on down.

An hour later Simon was in *Joe's Fight Gym* warming up on the heavy bag.

Ethan was working the focus pads with another black guy in one of the boxing rings.

As Simon got into a rhythm, he began moving around the bag putting together swift punch combinations as if he had been born to box.

He had no idea what he was going to throw next. It was as if Eddie Prince was guiding him through each move.

Soon, some of the other people training in the gym stopped to watch what could only be described as a masterful workout on the bag.

Simon was oblivious to them.

They were many admiring glances and whispered praise.

Ethan looked over from the ring and witnessed this.

When he had finished his training, he jumped out of the ring and headed over to Simon who was still punching away.

'Hey, champ. You are looking mean, boy,' Ethan said.

Simon looked up from the bag.

'Hello, Ethan. How are you?'

'Not as good as you, brother. Now what was all that bullshit about you never boxing? You hit that bag like a fucking pro.'

Simon laughed.

'I told you. I couldn't box eggs. This is Eddie Prince doing this.'

Ethan raised his eyebrows.

'Not all this Voodoo shit again, man.'

'Look, I have found some stuff out since we last met. Let's clean up and find somewhere private to talk,' said Simon.

Thirty minutes later, they were sat on a wooden bench in a small park a short walk from the gym.

As Nathan shook and mixed up his protein shake, he said, 'Alright man, spill the beans.'

Simon glanced around to see that there was nobody in ear shot.

'Firstly, I have found out 100% that Eddie Prince was the donor of my heart.'

Ethan stopped the shaking of his protein mixer.

'Shit, man. That is fucking incredible.'

Simon nodded.

'Yes, it is, and it backs up everything I have been feeling and everything I have told you.'

Ethan remained silent.

'Next, I have been to London to chat to a close friend of Eddie's when he lived there.

This man knew him well and told me part of the reason Eddie left London was because he owed a large debt to a local money lender. Archie Castle. A nasty bastard.

This man was tortured by Castle to Eddie's whereabouts.

He is positive Castle is the mystery shooter that murdered Eddie.'

Nathan let out a slow whistle.

'Fuck, man. That is some heavy shit you are telling me.'

Simon carried on.

'The splitting pain I was getting in my forehead was exactly where Eddie was shot. Plus, the visions I have been getting for months of an unknown man are now clear. That man was Archie Castle.'

Ethan interrupted him.

'How the hell can you be sure of that?'

'Because...' Simon answered, '...when I was up in London, I went into a bookmakers and this man was in there. He even gave me this card, telling me if I needed to lend money to come and see him.'

Ethan put up a hand.

'Now, wait a second. Let me get this right. Are you telling me because you have Eddie's heart that he somehow has been sending you messages about his killer and taking over your body and personality?'

Simon nodded.

'That about cuts it. Yes.'

Ethan shook his head.

'Do you know how crazy that makes you sound. This is like something out of a fucking horror film man.

'Ethan, look at all the evidence. It adds up. As crazy as it seems, it adds up.

Eddie went to an early grave. Taken by surprise. His heart, though, got used to save me and somehow there is memory there to what happened to him, and he was somehow translating it to me.'

'Alright. Let's say everything you told me is true. What does Eddie expect you to do about it?'

Simon was quiet for a moment.

'It has taken me a time to figure it out, Ethan. But essentially, Simon Winter died on that operating table. His life was over. He is only now alive because of Eddie, and he owes Eddie that.'

Ethan looked puzzled.

'I don't get what you are saying, man.'

Simon took a deep breath.

'Basically, Eddie wants me to find his killer.'

'Okay. So, you have done that. Now what? You have no hard evidence and from the sound of this guy you aren't going to get him to court any time soon. Plus, you walk into a police station with this story, and they will fucking lock you up.'

'I know all that, Ethan.'

'So, what is this all about Simon.'

'I am going to kill this motherfucker, so Eddie can rest in peace and so can I.'

Ethan nearly choked on a mouthful of shake.

'You are fucking what?'

'You heard me, Ethan.

Now can you get hold of a gun for me?'

Ethan jumped up from the bench.

'What the fuck are you talking about, man? Who do you think you are? The fucking equaliser? Have you totally lost the plot?'

Simon grabbed Ethan's arm.

'Sit the fuck down a minute, will you, and stop drawing attention to yourself.'

Ethan pulled his arm away and sat back down on the bench.

Simon regarded him.

'Listen to me, Ethan. I should be dead but somehow, I got another chance. But I have inherited a life that is not mine. Don't get me wrong, there were parts I loved. The new fitness and weight loss, becoming a hit with the ladies and overcoming my fears, particularly of violence and blood. Also, my newfound confidence.

But at the same time, Simon Winter's whole personality was being hijacked by the stronger personality of Eddie Prince. I have been living my life like a schizophrenic. I have no control over the mood changes. When I become Eddie, I am fucking dangerous.

Since I got his heart, he has been sending me messages about who killed him, and it is driving me insane. I have to finish this once and for all to claim any of my own life back.'

Ethan looked at Simon and saw the pain in his eyes.

'Look, man, if you go up against this Castle dude, you are fucked. He is a hardcore gangster, and you are a fucking estate agent. What do you plan to do? Give him a quote on a new flat in the Docklands and hopes he dies of shock from the price? Have you gone mad? You will die, man.'

Simon looked off in the direction of the lake.

'Maybe I am dead already. I am going to do this with or without your help, Ethan.'

Ethan stood up.

'I am not going to be personally responsible for you ending up like Eddie. I will not get you a firearm.'

'Ethan, I will get one from somebody else then. I am doing this.'

Ethan made to walk off but stopped and turned back to Simon.

'You don't just walk around asking any dodgy bastard you come across in a pub if they can get hold of a gun for you. This is serious shit, man.'

Simon regarded Ethan.

'If I got to, then I will. I am not going back on my word. Don't you want to see this bastard repaid for killing your best mate? Do you want him to get away with it? Nobody is interested. The police aren't going to re-open the case. Castle thinks he has got away scot-free. I have to do this. It is as if I was saved from dying to carry out this task. Simon Winter has always lived his life like a lamb. Now it is time for him to live it like a lion. Please help me.'

Ethan looked to the skies in frustration.

'Fucking hell, Simon. You are busting my balls, man. You are really serious about this. Aren't you?'

Simon nodded.

'Yes, I am, Ethan.'

Ethan leant in close to Simon.

'Back at the gym. Jock McBride who works behind reception, he can sort you. I will give him your mobile number and he will contact you.'

Simon stood up also.

'Thank you.'

He offered his hand forward.

Ethan ignored it.

'Don't call me again and stay away from the gym and the club. I have had my brushes with the law in the past and that's where I want to keep them. In the past.

My mum and dad are both seriously ill and I need to be about for them. I don't need to be involved in any dodgy shit. I have a good life these days. I don't want to end up back in prison.'

'That won't happen, Ethan. I swear it. If anything goes wrong, you will not be implicated in any way. You have my word,' replied Simon.

'Is that right? When all is said and done, I hardly know you, man. I don't know if your word means shit. Just for the record, I miss Eddie every day, but I will not be part of your madness. Goodbye.'

Ethan turned and this time walked away.

Simon watched him go.

He didn't blame him. If the shoe were on the other foot, he probably would be thinking like him.

A cold breeze suddenly wiped up that sent a shiver through Simon's body. He zipped up his jacket and walked back to his car.

The die was now cast. There would be no going back.

CHAPTER TWENTY THREE

Back at his flat that evening at 9.00pm, Simon received the call from Jock that he had been waiting for.

Dougie 'Jock' McBride asked Simon what gun he was looking for. Simon had done his research and asked for a Glock 17 with two ammunition clips.

The Scotsman wasn't fazed by the request and told him the cash price. He didn't ask any more questions and Simon never told him anything else.

Jock told Simon to meet him in the gym at 10.30pm. Everybody else would be gone by then and he would be locking up.

When Simon put his mobile down, his hands were shaking.

Simon waited in his car across the road from the gym. He saw the last few stragglers leaving the premises and waited until 10.30pm on the dot and then drove into the car park.

As he got out of his car, he saw Jock standing at the gym doorway. He didn't seem any less intimidating than the last time Simon saw him.

As Simon got nearer, Jock spoke, 'You got the money?'

Simon patted his jacket pocket.

'You got the merchandise?'

Jock nodded.

'Aye. Come in.'

Once Simon was inside Jock locked the door and pulled down the blinds.

He went behind the counter and returned with a Tesco carrier bag.

He opened the bag and took out the gun wrapped in a yellow cotton duster.

Simon watched as Jock unwrapped the gun and lay it on the table along with the two magazine clips.

Simon unzipped his jacket pocket and pulled out an envelope stuffed with cash.

Jock took it and counted the money.

When he was satisfied it was all there, he shoved it into his own coat pocket.

'It's unmarked and untraceable. When you have finished with it, I suggest you throw it in the water somewhere. You never got it from me, and we have never fucking met. Understand?'

Simon nodded.

Jock regarded him.

'Both clips hold 17 bullets. You ever used a Glock before?'

Simon shook his head.

'No'.

His throat felt dry.

Jock picked up the gun and ran through its workings and how to load it.

'They are reasonably lightweight and reliable. If you are near to your target, you will have a job not to hit them. Even an amateur like you should be okay.'

Simon picked up the gun and felt its weight. He looked at the imposing sleek barrel before rewrapping it and putting it with the clips back into the bag.

'Thanks.'

Jock moved to the door and pulled up the blind and looked outside. He then unlocked it.

As Simon walked past, 'Jock' said.

'Will I be reading about you in the newspaper any time soon?'

Simon smiled nervously.

'Who knows? Maybe.'

Jock's steely gaze never changed.

'Go on. Fuck off and remember we never met.'

Simon drove home carefully. The last thing he needed was to be pulled over by the police with a gun in the boot of his car.

He felt like an outlaw. Never in his wildest dreams would he have thought he ever would own a handgun. Fuck, he wasn't living in Texas. But here he was locked and loaded literally.

It was as if some unseen force was guiding him, and this force was getting stronger every day.

The old Simon Winter would never have contemplated what he was going to do, but this wasn't the Simon of old.

He now realised that this person was nearly non-existent as the personality of Eddie Prince had now consumed him.

His only thought was revenge. Nothing else mattered.

When he got home to his flat, he shut and locked the front door.

He took the gun from the bag and unwrapped it and sat it on the coffee table with the two clips.

Simon suddenly had the desire for a drink.

There wasn't much in the house in the way of alcohol as it was usually only Andrea who drank it.

He rummaged in a kitchen cupboard and found a half empty bottle of gin.

He grabbed a glass and poured a generous measure. There was no tonic that he could find so he cut up a slice of lemon to go in it.

Simon brought it back to the sofa and sat down and took a gulp.

He wasn't sure whether he liked it or not.

Funny as years back he would have drunk any spirit put down in front of him.

Putting the glass down on the coffee table, he picked up the gun.

He felt its weight and found himself racking it, checking the safety and loading and unloading a clip with an expertise he didn't know he possessed until now.

Once again, he felt he was having an outer body experience and it was somebody else doing this.

Simon finished his drink in two more mouthfuls and headed to the bedroom, bringing the gun with him.

Once in the bedroom, he stood in front of the full-length wardrobe mirror and struck a shooting pose with the gun.

Fucking hell, he felt like James Bond.

Standing close to the mirror, he then moved into his best impersonation of Robert De Niro's character Travis Bickle in the cult film *Taxi Driver.*

'You looking at me? I said, you looking at me?'

Simon grinned.

He next tucked the gun into his waistband and practised drawing it and levelling it.

At first, he fumbled the move, but a couple of dozen more attempts down the line, he was getting better.

He was engrossed in what he was doing. Focused on a smooth draw. He visualised the scene in his head that he wanted.

As he drew and levelled again, he looked forward and, for a fleeting moment, the reflection in the mirror wasn't his. It was Eddie Prince looking back holding the shooting stance. A small smile played on his lips, and he nodded his head in an act of acknowledgement.

Simon froze momentarily and turned away to look around the room. When he looked back again, the image in the mirror was gone and it was only him staring back.

Putting the gun down on the bed beside him as he sat down, he noticed that he was sweating and there was a slight tremor in his hands.

What the fuck had just happened there?

That had been far too real for him to have imagined it.

Simon stood up and shed his clothes. He decided to have a shower.

As he passed the wardrobe, he gingerly glanced at the mirror.

It was only his reflection that he saw.

When Simon finished his shower, he put on his dressing gown and began to get ready for this trip to London. He had no idea if he would ever return to this flat and this life.

He packed a suitcase with clothes and toiletries. He put the gun and ammo in the bottom.

He looked around the flat that he had lived in since he separated from his wife and realised there was nothing of a sentimental nature in it.

There were materialistic things, such as books, CDS, DVDs and a handful of computer games, but they weren't important.

He went to a bedside cabinet and found his passport. He would take it as insurance.

In his sock and underwear drawer, he retrieved a roll of money that he had been using for his gambling stakes.

He left behind his wallet with his bank and credit cards, plus driver's license in it.

He was making this trip incognito.

Earlier that day, he had bought a burner phone with cash. No trace back to him. He had keyed in only a few essential phone numbers.

He realised there weren't many people of importance in his life. He had lots of acquaintances, but no real friends.

He thought of Andrea and agonised over whether he should leave a note for her.

What would he say?

Off for a weekend's shooting. See you Monday.

He decided in the end not to bother.

Who could tell how things would go?

He might decide to come back and be there Monday morning with a breakfast of blueberry pancakes, Andrea's favourite, when she walked through the door from a long flight.

She would never know.

His alias would be hidden like a comic book superhero.

Simon Winter, crimebuster and righter of wrongs.

Simon had loved to read those comics when he was younger and had envisaged himself as Spiderman or Daredevil. Changing from a mild-mannered college student or lawyer into a living, breathing ass-kicking machine.

Those comics had comforted him from the bullies in his life.

His eye then caught a framed photograph on top of the dressing table of his children.

Harry and Chloe were both smiling with the beach and blue sea of Majorca behind them.

The image had been taken last year on their summer holiday with Jean and Tommy.

The kids had sent it to him, and he had got it printed from his phone in Asda and got it framed.

He felt a pang of guilt inside, but the truth was they were both happy with their new life. Daddy was no longer essential in their daily habits.

Jean had filed for a divorce, and she wanted to marry Tommy.

She had told Simon recently when that happened that they were all going to re-locate up to Cumbria where Tommy had been born.

His parents, who had passed on some months ago, had left him the family home seeing he was their only child.

A four-bedroom stone cottage with land.

How could he deny her or the children this? He had been a lousy husband and Dad. Even if he contested it, he wouldn't have a leg to stand on.

Simon wiped a tear from his eye.

It was no time for sentiment.

He had a job to do.

He planned to drive to London first thing in the morning. He had booked a room under a false name at a Travelodge and once more he would pay cash when he arrived.

It was nearly 1.00am when he slid under the sheets of his bed. He lay in the darkness staring at the ceiling listening to the ticking of the bedside clock. As he suspected, sleep wasn't going to come easy.

Finally, in the small hours, he drifted off.

Simon walked through a thick mist. He was in London, but it looked like the streets of Victorian London. Whitechapel. Jack the Ripper territory.

In the shrouded darkness behind him, he could hear footsteps following.

Whenever Simon turned around, the footsteps stopped.

Panic rose in his chest, and he felt his heart rate increasing.

He couldn't see his hand in front of his face. It was a real peasouper.

He was lost and somebody was pursuing him.

He reached for his waist band and comfortingly touched the handgun.

It made him feel a little better.

He had come to London to find someone, but now the hunter had become the hunted.

How had things gone so wrong?

Simon stumbled as he walked into a rubbish bin.

He nearly lost his footing, but managed to stay upright.

Although the air was bitterly cold, he found himself sweating profusely and his breathing was laboured.

He needed to keep moving and find a familiar landmark. But London was not his home.

Suddenly, up ahead he saw a blue light shining brightly out of the gloom.

As he got closer, he realised it was the Travelodge that he was staying at.

Thank God.

He began to run and the footsteps behind him also ran.

Simon kept heading for the light. The beacon of safety.

But as hard and fast as he ran, it just seemed agonisingly out of reach.

A sudden sharp pain in his chest brought him to a halt.

The vice-like grip on his sternum caused him to drop to his knees in agony.

This was it. His new heart was giving up on him. He was going to die.

The mist then began to clear and whoever had been following him came into view.

*'Help me, please. Call an ambulance!' asked Simon.
His voice almost a whisper.*

*As the person got closer, Simon saw to his horror
that it was Archie Castle.*

*Castle bent in close, and Simon could smell whisky
on the man's breath.*

*'Hello, son, you don't look too good. A bit pale, to
tell the truth.'*

Simon closed his eyes as the pain got worse.

'An ambulance. Quick. I am dying.'

Castle grinned.

'Indeed you are. Now let me help you on your way.'

*Simon saw Castle produce a gun from his coat and
pointed it at his head.*

*'Time to leave this planet, you interfering little
bastard. Just like your pal Eddie Prince.'*

*Simon was powerless to do anything as the gun was
fired.*

Simon sat bolt upright in bed, his hands automatically
clutching at his head checking for blood. It took him a
moment to realise he had been having another
nightmare.

It was just a bad dream. Nothing more.

He was safe.

As his breathing began to decrease, he lay back
down.

Any more sleep was definitely out of the question.

He lay awake until the early morning light shone
into his bedroom.

CHAPTER TWENTY FOUR

Simon

So, here I am in London. I booked into my accommodation without any problem. The Travelodge had an underground car park, which was very convenient. My car is tucked out of the way safely.

I won't be needing it for now. I am going to be on foot. Much easier to blend in with London's workers and tourists.

I am sat on the bed in my room sipping a cup of tea. I feel strangely calm.

Beside me on the duvet is Archie Castle's business card.

I pick it up and dial the number on my mobile.

I wait to be connected.

The time is 4.00pm.

I left Bristol this morning at 10.00am and got to my destination around 12.30pm.

Apart from a few roadworks on the M5 outside Reading, it had been a pretty smooth journey.

I parked up in the underground car park and paid the 24-hour fee.

I couldn't get into my room until after 3.00pm so I took a walk to find Castle's night club, *Lacey's.*

I found it after a 20-minute walk in a side street of Soho.

I walked past the building casually, trying not to bring too much notice to myself.

The façade was all purples and blacks. The windows had dark tinted glass and the front door was solid metal.

I noticed a security camera above it facing out onto the road.

A sign hung up high above the windows with the silhouettes of two naked woman dancing on it.

Very tasteful.

I then walked around the block to the rear of the building but could not see much due to a high brick wall.

It wasn't going to be the best exit point if it came to it.

After this quick scan of the place, I headed back to the Travelodge.

I took out my phone and rang Castle's number.

On the fifth ring, the phone connected, but it went to an answerphone.

A recorded voice of a woman stated that the club was at present shut and to leave your name, number and a short message and somebody would get back to you.

I was prepared for this.

I gave my name as Simon White and my mobile number.

I went on to explain that I had been given a business card by Mr. Castle in connection with a loan.

I hung up the call.

My adrenaline was rising as I had now played my final card.

It was down to a waiting game now.

Exactly 15 minutes later, my phone rang.

I answered it.

'Hello.'

A gruff male voice spoke.

'Is this Simon White?'

'Yes,' I replied.

My heart was hammering in my chest.

'You asked to speak to Mr. Castle about a loan?'

'That's right. He gave me his card in a bookie's a little while ago and told me to call him if I needed money.'

'What was the name of the bookie's you met in?'

'It was near Leicester Square. I think it was a branch of Safe Bet next door to a KFC.'

The phone went silent, and, for a moment, I thought the man had gone.

Then he spoke again.

'Come to the club tomorrow morning at 10.30am. Knock on the door and when the intercom buzzes, announce yourself and your business. Be punctual. Mr. Castle is a busy man and doesn't tolerate lateness. Understand?'

I swallowed hard and kept my voice even.

'I understand. I will be there.'

The phone went dead.

I lay back on the bed and breathed a sigh of relief. *Game on.*

Later, I went and grabbed some food at a McDonalds. I hadn't been in one since my transplant, but I needed somewhere where I could just blend in and not have to book into a restaurant.

I sat at a window table and began to eat my McChicken sandwich. I had a flashback to the time

I saw my old mate Greg Badcock sat at the window of a McDonalds not long before he passed away.

It seemed a lifetime away now.

My whole life before my transplant was becoming a distant memory.

In recent days inside my head, I could hear Eddie speaking to me. Guiding me. Giving me confidence to perform my task.

I couldn't go back if I tried. His influence was now too strong to fight.

My thoughts returned to the club. There was no way I would get into that place tomorrow without being searched. My gun would be found, and it would be all over.

So, I decided that I would go to the club tonight and somehow find a way to smuggle the gun inside the premises and then hide it. I thought the toilets would be a good bet.

Tomorrow when I entered the club, I would make an excuse to use the toilets and then retrieve the gun and finish the job.

It was as good a plan as I could think of. I had nothing else.

I just had to figure out how to smuggle a gun into the place tonight.

That was going to be the hard bit.

I needed to come up with something soon as the clock was ticking.

Back at the Travelodge, I used their Wi-Fi station to check what times *Lacey's* opened and closed.

The place was a strip joint, lap dance and nightclub all rolled into one.

The strip show was normally from 10.00pm to 12.00am.

Lap dancing was in private rooms.

The nightclub opened for music at 1.00am and closed at 5.00am

I went back out and headed to *Lacey's*. I needed another look at the place.

It was still all closed.

There was no activity whatsoever.

Still too early for staff to arrive.

I stood on the other side of the road with my mobile to my ear pretending to be having a conversation.

I was dressed down in dark tracksuit bottoms and a dark outdoor trekking jacket. I wore a black beanie pulled tightly down on my head.

Any CCTV in the vicinity wouldn't be able to clearly identify me.

I studied the outside of the club.

The entrance had a couple of steps leading up to the front door.

There was nothing else outside the building.

A little way down the road was a bus shelter and next to it was a lamp post with a metal waste bin attached to it.

This interested me.

I walked over to the bus stop and made a pretence of studying the faded timetable that hung there.

On the bench that ran along the length of the shelter stood a solitary empty can of Carlsberg Special Brew.

I picked it up and brought it to the waste bin and put it in there. I noticed the bin was full to the top.

Hopefully, it would not be emptied this late in the day.

A plan began to formulate in my head.

On the way back to the Travelodge, I stopped in a newsagent and bought 20 Lambert and Butlers and a Zippo lighter. It had been a long time since I bought cigarettes.

Once back at my accommodation, I had time on my hands yet so I decided to see if I could take a nap. It was going to be a late night.

Surprisingly, I dozed off quite quickly.

I was awoken sometime later by the alarm I had set on the digital beside clock.

It was 10.30pm and dark in the room.

I lay for a few moments to compose my thoughts and then got up, put on the light and drew the curtains together.

I brewed myself a mug of tea from the complimentary tray.

My stomach growled.

I found a protein bar in my case, which I bought earlier at a service station. I wolfed it down hungrily.

After, I went and had a long hot shower.

I took my time washing and shampooed my hair.

Once dry, I went to my suitcase and pulled out my best blue suit.

I wanted to dress smart to get into the nightclub.

I blow-dried my hair and groomed my beard and splashed on some aftershave.

Studying myself in the mirror, I was satisfied with my appearance.

I put £150.00, my mobile and my room key in my pockets.

I didn't need anything else tonight.

Just another punter on a Friday night out for a good time on the town.

In my case, I pulled out a pair of surgical gloves and slipped them on.

I next wiped the gun and ammo clips clean.

I then wrapped them inside a couple of Tesco bags along with the gloves.

I now checked around the room and switched off the light and left discreetly.

There was nobody on the reception as I walked out the front door.

When I reached the bus shelter again, I was relieved to find it empty. I glanced up the road to the club and there was a queue of people lined up to go inside. None of them were showing me any interest, so I put the carrier bag with the gun and ammo inside into the bin under a couple of empty cardboard Big Mac boxes. I prayed they would be safe until later.

Once I had done this, I walked up the road and joined the line for *Lacey's*.

Looking around at the other people in the queue, I felt old. Most of them must have been in their twenties. I felt a little out of place.

The line started moving and I had no time for second thoughts.

As I neared the front, I ran my eyes over the two door personnel overseeing people going in.

As I suspected, they were searching everybody before letting them inside.

Both the men were white and by their accents from Eastern Europe. They both had the build of powerlifters and all the charm of a pair of rottweilers.

I guessed they weren't employed for their good looks and sparkling repartee.

Once I reached the front of the line, one of the men ran a hand-held metal detector over me.

When satisfied I wasn't carrying anything dangerous, he nodded for me to go inside.

As I entered the dark interior, I was greeted by the thump of loud music, which seemed to vibrate through my very being.

I didn't know the music being played as my knowledge of dance tunes stopped with the Bee Gees and *Saturday Night Fever.*

The place was filling up quickly.

To my right was the dance floor and to my left a long, well-stocked bar.

In the centre of the room was a raised platform where an animated guy in dark shades and a baseball cap performed his magic on the music decks.

The name lit up below him in neon lettering read *Cheeky Cal Cummins.*

Whatever happened to good old Tony Blackburn?

I moved to the bar and ordered a whisky and coke.

It was more for appearance's sake than drinking.

I needed a clear head.

I estimated I had to hang around in here for an hour or so before I made my next move.

I stood at the bar and turned to face the dance floor.

I tapped my foot and moved my head as if I were into the grooves.

Lots of hot young flesh twisted and gyrated to the music.

Christ, I did feel I was getting older by the second.

Beyond the bar, I could see the toilets.

I paid them a visit and checked out their layout.

Coming back out, I noticed a short corridor to my left.

It was chained off and marked private.

Beyond it, I saw a door marked "Office".

I suspected that was where I would have to go tomorrow to meet Castle.

A shiver went through my body and, for a moment, I asked myself what the fuck had I got into?

Then Eddie's voice hi-jacked my thoughts.

Don't go doubting yourself now. You are nearly there. Stay strong.

The feeling of unease left me, and I walked back to the bar.

I stood once again looking out to the dance floor biding my time.

Suddenly, I was aware of the presence of somebody stood close by my side.

I glanced to my left and there was a pretty red-haired girl. Young enough to probably be my daughter.

'Hi, I am Phoebe. Do you want to buy me a drink?'

I was taken aback by her directness.

'Hello, Phoebe, I am Simon. Now why would a gorgeous young girl like yourself be hitting on a middle-aged man like me?'

Phoebe smiled slyly.

'Can't a girl fancy an older man?'

I laughed.

'Normally there is a catch in it. You are welcome to a drink, but we will leave it at that.'

Phoebe tutted.

'Oh, alright then. I will have a G&T please.'

I ordered the drink.

'So, what's the real story?'

Phoebe took a sip of her drink.

'It's my prick of a boyfriend. We just had an argument on the dance floor because he was eying up some tart.

He stormed off to the toilet and I came over here for a drink but remembered he had all the money.'

'Well, I admire your candour. Would this be him now striding towards us?'

Phoebe looked in the direction I had nodded.

'Yes. That's him. Dopey Darren.'

By the look of his body language, Darren wasn't coming over to shake hands.

He postured up in front of me.

'What the fuck are you doing with my girlfriend?'

I coolly sipped my drink and eyed him up.

I estimated he was in his early 20s. He still had the zits to prove it.

He was tall and lanky and seemed to like his tattoos that adorned his arms up to where they disappeared under his short-sleeved shirt.

'I was doing nothing with your girlfriend. I am just stood at the bar minding my own business.'

A sneer spread over his face.

'Is that right? I saw you buy her a drink.'

'No law against that, is there?'

Darren stepped forward and got in my face. I could smell vodka on his breath.

'Well, you can fuck off now, Dad, and mind your own business. Understand?'

As Darren said this, he poked me in the chest.

I hated that. So many bullies in the past had done that to me.

I could hear Eddie Prince inside my head again.

'Chin the little shit. Don't let him fuck with you.'

As much as I wanted to, I couldn't afford to make a scene in the club. It would spoil my plan if I got myself chucked out.

I sucked it in.

'Loud and clear, man. I am off outside anyway for a smoke.'

Darren smiled, his confidence now skyrocketing.

'Yeah. You do that, Dad, and don't fucking come back.'

I walked to the door keeping a rein on Eddie's anger.

You should have knocked him out.

When I got outside, I lit up a cigarette and stood on the step and inhaled the smoke.

For a minute, I thought I might cough my lungs up, but I recovered.

I nodded acknowledgement to both the doormen.

One of them eyed me and then said, 'Have you got a spare one of those?'

'Sure,' I answered.

I gave him a cigarette and lit it for him.

He acknowledged this.

'Thank you, my friend.'

He went back to talking to his colleague and I casually walked down the street a little, then pulled out my phone on the pretence of making a call.

I looked back. Both men were not paying me any attention.

I walked straight up to the bin. The bus shelter was still empty. I put my phone away.

It took me seconds to reach in and retrieve the bag.

I brought it around to the back of the bus shelter and opened it. I fished out the gloves and pulled them on. Next, I took out the gun and clips and slipped them into one of my jacket pockets. I stuffed the bag in another and pulled off the gloves, also pocketing them.

I began to walk back to the club, talking into my phone once again.

As I reached the door, I said in a loud voice, 'I will be home when I am good and ready. Now don't call me anymore.'

I looked up at the two doormen.

'Bloody women. What a fucking pain in the ass they are.'

The two men laughed and acknowledged my statement.

I dropped the remains of my smoke on the pavement and ground it out with the heel of my shoe and walked straight back into the club.

Sweet.

Once inside, I walked towards the toilets.

I pushed the door open to the gents.

A couple of guys stood at the urinals.

I also noted one of the stall doors was shut.

I went to one of the vacant urinals and waited for the other two to finish.

Once they left, I headed to the toilet stall furthest away from the one in use.

I locked the door and pulled on my gloves and took out the carrier bag and put the gun and clips back inside.

I wrapped it all up tightly and placed it on the closed-down toilet seat.

I now silently removed the top of the cistern.

Next, I picked up the bag and stuffed it down into the water.

The weight kept it at the bottom of the cistern. I then replaced the top and hoped and prayed it would be there waiting for me tomorrow.

I left the stall and went to the sinks to wash my hands.

The door of the occupied toilet then opened and who should walk out but 'Dopey Darren'.

His eyes lit up when he saw me.

'Well, look who it is! I thought I told you to fuck off out of it.'

I was now tired, and my job was done here.

I was alone with this jerk. The tables had now turned in my favour.

It was time to let Eddie off the leash for a little while.

About fucking time.

I turned around to face Darren.

'Listen, son. Here is a bit of advice for you. Earlier in front of your girlfriend, I let you save face.

Now it is different. I suggest you walk away and leave me alone.'

The stupid smirk was back on the kid's face again.

'Oh yeah. Or what, Dad?'

I moved with the speed of a panther and closed the distance on Darren in a heartbeat.

I gripped the boy by the testicles and squeezed hard before driving him back into the toilet stall he had come out of a moment ago.

Darren slammed up against a wall.

The fear in the boy's bulging eyes was apparent.

'Right, you little shit. This is your last warning, and you better listen good.'

To emphasise my point, I squeezed his balls harder.

'I chose earlier not to blast you off the planet and at this moment I am finding it hard to choose not to do it again. So, get the fuck out of here and leave me alone or I will fucking hurt you badly. Understand?'

Darren nodded dumbly as tears ran down his cheeks from the pain.

I let him go and he sagged to the toilet floor.

All his youthful bluff and bravado had gone.

He looked a sorry sight.

I walked back over to the sinks, rewashed my hands and fixed my hair in the mirror.

Satisfied, I turned towards the door as two men walked in.

I glanced towards the stall and Darren was still on his ass watching me like a young gazelle would eye a prowling lion.

Hopefully, he had learnt a valuable lesson this evening.

As I walked back into the club, I saw Phoebe at the bar.

I walked past her.

'If you are wondering why Darren is so long in the toilet, he is feeling a little under the weather. Nice meeting you, Phoebe. If you want a little advice, get rid of that clown. You can do better.'

Before she could answer, I walked out into the cold night air.

My two friends were still holding vigil on the door.

'Good night, gentlemen,' I said as I walked off into the night.

The trap was now baited. Next, I had to spring it.

CHAPTER TWENTY FIVE

Simon got back to his room at 3.30am. He was wired and knew that going to bed at present would be a waste of time.

He brewed a mug of tea and flicked through the television channels in hope of finding something to watch.

On one of the Freeview channels, he found one of his favourite films, *Jaws*.

It had only just started so he began to watch it for the umpteenth time. He never tired of it.

By the time the final credits were rolling, his eyes had become heavy.

He checked his watch. The time was now 5.45am.

Simon set the alarm on the bedside clock once more and settled down on the bed for two hours sleep.

His dreams were muddled as he saw Eddie Prince sitting at his bedside. He was smiling at him, even though he had a bullet hole between his eyes.

I told him that redemption was near and that I was ready to claim it for him.

Eddie then ripped open his shirt to reveal his open chest cavity minus his heart.

Then he was replaced by Archie Castle.

Castle was smoking a cigar. His malevolent smile chilled Simon's blood.

He then spoke.

'*You are out of your depth, son. Well out of it. You are about to make the biggest mistake of your life.*'

As Castle disappeared, he was replaced by Ethan.

'*Come back home, brother. You don't have to do this. Eddie is dead. This won't bring him back. Give up this madness and come home.*'

Simon finally saw movie actor Roy Scheider who played Chief Brody in *Jaws* shaking his head at him and utter the immortal words.

'*You are going to need a bigger boat.*'

The alarm woke Simon from his troubled sleep with a start.

His heart was pumping fast, and his body was bathed in sweat.

He lay for a few moments composing himself.

Simon then got up and headed for the shower to wash away the remnants of his sleep.

Simon

I am ready. I am a few moments away from *Lacey's*. My adrenaline is bubbling in my bloodstream. My whole body feels like a car sat at the traffic lights with the handbrake on and the driver pumping the accelerator pedal but going nowhere.

The slow dripping tap of adrenaline I had been living with for days was now becoming a flow.

I breathed deeply.

I knew the adrenaline was my friend, but I needed to be its master and not the other way around.

I needed detached icy calm, not burning fire.

I had to act with my head and not my heart, if you excuse the pun.

The only problem was it wasn't my heart, but a dead man's hell bent on revenge.

I felt I was losing the battle to control Eddie, but I needed to stay in control for what I was about to do.

If I let emotion come into play, I was surely a dead man.

I prayed I could keep Eddie at bay.

I walked up to the front door of the club and as instructed, knocked on it on the dot of 10.30am.

An intercom crackled and the same gruff voice I heard on the phone yesterday answered.

'Yes.'

I breathed deeply once more to keep the quaver out of my voice.

'This is Simon White. I have a 10.30am appointment with Mr. Castle about a loan. I rang yesterday and booked it.'

A buzzer sounded and the door was opened.

The owner of the gruff voice turned out to be a large black guy with an impressive head of dreadlocks.

He reminded me of Bob Marley on steroids.

'Come in,' he instructed me.

Once over the threshold, he locked the door and then told me to put my arms out and stand still.

I complied as he bodysearched me.

Satisfied, he told me to follow him, and we walked through the club.

Now quiet and empty, it seemed a different place than last night.

The place smelt faintly of alcohol, sweat and polish.

A small group of cleaners were just finishing up their work.

I was led through to the corridor I saw last night just past the toilets.

'Wait here while I see if the boss is ready to see you.' 'Rasta' told me.

I nodded.

'Is it alright if I can quickly use the toilet? Too much coffee this morning.'

'Rasta' eyed me suspiciously for a moment.

'Go on then but be quick. If the Boss is ready, he isn't a man to keep waiting.'

'Thanks,' I replied, 'I won't be a minute.'

As the black man disappeared down the corridor towards the office, I hurriedly headed for the toilets.

Once inside, I was relieved to find it empty. No cleaners.

I went into the last urinal and closed the door before lifting the top of the cistern off.

Looking in, I saw the bag was still there.

I quickly retrieved it and unwrapped the gun and ammo clips.

I pocketed one clip.

I now racked the slide and cleared it, catching it open on the slide catch.

Next, I put a magazine into the handle and released the catch. The slide went back, and the gun was ready to fire.

I noticed the slight tremor in my hands as I put it into the waistband of my trousers at the small of my back.

This was it.

Eddie's voice suddenly sounded in my head.

You are ready. Remember, control and detachment. Do the job and get out.

I pulled the flush and came out of the cubicle.

I was surprised to see the black guy stood there.

'Let's go. The boss is ready.'

I walked towards the door.

'Wait,' said 'Rasta'.

I froze. What the fuck had he seen?

I held my breath in anticipation.

'Haven't you forgot something?' he asked.

I was confused.

'I don't think so.'

The black man nodded towards the sink.

'Wash your hands. Fucking hygiene, man.'

I smiled weakly and did as he said.

Once outside the office door, 'Rasta' spoke again.

'When you go inside, speak when you're spoken to and do not interrupt.

If you are borrowing money, be clear on how much you want and if you sign the paperwork, don't question it. Understand?'

'Yes. I understand.'

I tried to look calm, but I was performing what is known as the *Duck Syndrome*.

This is where you observe a duck gliding effortless along the top of a pond where under the water, unseen by you, its little legs are going like hell.

Inside, my body was having a meltdown but, on the outside, I was doing everything in my power to look calm.

Eddie whispered in my ear.

Breathe. Get a rein on it. Remember, you are the master. Control.

'Rasta' knocked the door, and it was opened by another big man.

He was white. He sported a green mohawk and an array of face piercing.

He must be the customer relations manager, I mused.

Once in the room, I quickly surveyed it.

There was a sofa to the left of me, occupied by another human mountain who was giving me a death stare.

Some shelving and bookcases to my right.

Centre stage was a large oak desk and behind it sat Archie Castle.

He was speaking into his mobile.

'You have three hours to come up with the scratch, you little prick, or my boys will come around your garage and set it alight and then they will dismantle you with a fucking chainsaw. So, I suggest, my son, you find the fucking money fast.'

Castle hung up and dropped his phone on the desk.

He then regarded me with beady eyes.

'You try and help some people and they just try to take advantage. I can't be doing with it.'

Castle opened an ornate book on his desk and reached inside, taking out a cigar.

As he put it between his lips, 'Mohawk' was by his side in a flash with a lighter.

Castle took a draw and blow a cloud of smoke up into the air.

'Cheers, Chris.'

He then gestured to a chair this side of his desk.

'Take a seat, Mr. White. Can I offer you a coffee, tea or something stronger?'

I sat down, praying the gun wouldn't work loose from my waistband.

'No, thank you, Mr. Castle. I am fine.'

Castle looked in the direction of the pit-bull on the sofa.

'Bas, get me a cappuccino, no sugar.'

The man extradited his huge bulk from the sofa and left the room.

'Right then, son. You want to take out a loan. Is that right?'

This was my moment to use surprise as my ally.

I couldn't wait any longer. The adrenaline build-up was killing me.

It was fight or flight time.

I answered him.

'No, that isn't what I came here for.'

Castle looked surprised.

'I don't get it.'

He now looked over to 'Rasta'.

'Leon, you took the phone call yesterday. What's going on?'

The black man looked confused.

Castle looked back at me.

'So, what is it you want?'

'I am not here for a loan. I am here to collect a debt.'

Castle broke into a laugh.

'I don't know who you are, son, but you have got some bollocks coming in here and talking like that.'

He gestured to his men.

'Get rid of this rubbish, will you? And give him a good few digs as well.'

Before either man could move, I jumped up and pulled the gun free.

'Don't fucking move, assholes.

The three men all had a look of shock on their faces as to how I could have got into the inner sanctum armed.

'What the fuck is all this?' snarled Castle.

'Remember Eddie Prince?'

Castle regarded me .

'The boxer Eddie Prince. Yeah, I remember him. What of it?'

I took a breath, trying to keep the emotion from my voice.

'You killed him, you cowardly bastard. Shot him from the backseat of your car. Gunned him down like a dog.'

'Eddie Prince was a dog. A thieving dog who deserved what he got.

So, what's your story? You want money, is that it? Well, you can go fuck yourself.

You haven't got what it takes to do this. I can tell. I can see it in your eyes.'

Just then the door opened, and Bas came in with the coffee.

That's when 'Mohawk' and 'Rasta' reached inside their jackets.

I turned and fired a shot that hit 'Rasta' squarely in the chest. The impact sent the man crashing back into the wall.

A bullet whizzed past my head into the bookcase behind me. I felt searing pain as the tip of my ear was blown off.

I turned to 'Mohawk', who was levelling the gun again, but I got my shot off first.

It hit him in the throat. The bullet tore out through the base of his skull, and he dropped to the floor instantly.

Castle was reaching into a desk drawer. I fixed my aim on him.

'Don't fucking move!' I screamed.

He froze.

I levelled my gun but that was when I was hit hard by Bas as he tackled me to the floor.

His head smashed into my chest.

The impact was like colliding with a truck.

It shook my internal organs. I instantly felt excruciating pain.

Every ounce of breath had been knocked out of my body.

He was on me instantly like a grizzly bear. Straddling my chest, his huge bulk crushing me.

Miraculously, I still had hold of my gun.

I smashed the butt end into his temple twice and he grunted, shifting his weight off me slightly.

There was now enough space for me to stick the barrel of the Glock under his chin and pull the trigger.

His head exploded in front of me like an overripe melon. I was covered in blood and gore.

I rolled his bulk off of me, but the pain in my chest almost made me pass out.

I suspected damaged to my breastbone and possibly my heart.

As I got to my knees, a shadow loomed over me.

'You crazy fuck. I don't know who you are to Prince, but you are going to die just like him.'

I tried to level my gun, but the pain slowed me down.

Castle fired his weapon and a bullet hit me in the stomach. I slumped back against the wall.

I saw Castle walk towards me grinning.

He was coming in for the kill.

'Time to say goodbye, asshole.'

I somehow summoned every ounce of strength left in my body and fired another shot.

My bullet ripped through his kneecap, causing his leg to buckle under him.

Castle dropped to his knees screaming. His gun fell from his fingers.

This gave me the chance to level my gun at his head.

My breath was coming in shallow gulps.

I regarded Castle's curled-up body on the floor.

'You might have been right that I don't have the bottle to do this, but Eddie Prince does.'

Castle looked up at me with confusion on his face.

I shot him directly between the eyes just as he had Eddie.

Leaning back against the wall, I dropped my gun.

It was done.

Eddie had got his revenge at last.

Blood began to pool around me.

The pain in my chest was also getting worse.

Time was slowing down and somewhere in the distance I heard sirens.

'We did it, Eddie. You and me. We did it.'

'We sure did Simon. Justice has been done. Time to rest now.'

I grimaced in pain as I began to fall in and out of consciousness from blood loss.

'I will see you on the other side, Eddie. Maybe grab a beer…'

Eddie is no longer answering.

My heart rate is slowing rapidly. Or should I say Eddie's?

Either way it doesn't matter. We have been one and the same person now for so long.

A sense of peace begins to wash over me.

I think of my kids. Then Jean, Andrea, Ester and Nathan.

What will they say when this all comes to light?

Hero or villain? Brave or stupid.

The sirens are closer now.
This is it, Eddie my old friend. Our time has come.

So much blood everywhere.

I now take one more look at the carnage before me. The dead bodies. The acrid smell of cordite and the coppery tang of blood.

How do I know these people around me are dead?

Because I have just killed them.

Yes, little old me.

I will let you into a secret. I enjoyed it.

I felt euphoric.

I have never had a feeling like that in my whole life.

Nothing compares or even comes close to it.

I am glad I experienced it.

I loved it with all my heart.

Ha. All my heart. How apt.

So much blood everywhere. Did I mention I used to hate blood...